# THE SEER

## A Novel

**C. Orville McLeish**

Published by:

Connect with the Author: www.corvillemcleish.com

This novel is a work of fiction. Names, characters, places, and incidents are either products of the author's imagination or used fictitiously. All characters are fictional, and any similarity to people living or dead is purely coincidental or maybe prophetic.

ISBN: 978-1-953759-82-5 (paperback)
ISBN: 978-1-953759-83-2 (eBook)

Printed in the United States of America.

*To all God's children…*
*You are the one.*

*To my wife, Nordia McLeish, who believes in me and supports my crazy journey.*

# Table of Contents

# Prologue

It's late spring in Minnesota, almost summer. It's bright and colorful in the afternoon, streets populated with pedestrians, some of them students excited for the summer, chatting animatedly, walking back home from school.

The sky is very blue and clear, only the occasional cloud floating by. Picnics in fields, kids playing, riding bikes, and chasing squirrels. It's an exceptionally lovely day to be outside.

Traffic moves as usual; the afternoon rush just ended, so the crush of cars on the highway is steadily trying to lessen. Honks and curses even though the traffic lights' red. It's a Tuesday, and several hours past lunchtime, the hubbub in several offices is back in full swing; discussions trying to override themselves, the shrill cries of telephones, printers, and scanners whirring in the background.

It's a lovely spring Tuesday. Some kids gang up in an alley against themselves, fighting over something insignificant. Bars are just opening and empty, but their alleyways have been operating since midnight. People exchange money under shirts—powder and other things that could get them arrested. Drunks are just starting to come to, squinting confused in the sunlight and frowning against the banging in their heads. Some of them just slouch back to the ground and wonder how everything had gone wrong.

In the heart of May, flowers blossom, birds fly, insects buzz around. It's a cool afternoon with great weather for plenty of pictures, a date, or even a confrontation with a rival.

Nature is in full bloom; the earth is flourishing. It's wonderful and normal; it's the earth. The world. The mortal realm. There is another world, more vast, without limits, without end, yet unseen to the physical eyes and ignored by the majority of the population.

The realm of light is a bright place filled with beautiful translucent beings. Its borders stretch without end, and its occupants multiply without cease. There is a hubbub, a collection of whispers passing between beings. They whisper and laugh, sing and play and dance. Here, spirits and souls, cherubs and seraphs and archangels mingle freely, existing in perfect spiritual harmony.

A soul, Paul, moves to where he can stare at the mortal realm.

It is majestic, the mortal realm, and magical. It was filled with everything and nothing. Beautiful things are living together. It was created with utmost care and perfect balance. But, its light grows dimmer with each orbit of the sun. Darkness shrouds its golden goodness, beams of light dispersed over its surface, desperately peaking out but obscured and dissipating below the spreading darkness.

Paul stares at the world, at the earth. He is concerned and fascinated by what he sees.

An angel, a seraph, comes to him, to stand by his side and stare too into the world.

"It looks…different," Paul replies.

"The darkness is spreading. Earth suffocates in its greed, aggression, and selfishness."

"From what I imagined, it is different. I've heard stories, but this…seems overwhelming…"

Below the realm of light, in the mortal realm, Cindy splashes in a puddle and squeals in delight. She's just turned seven last month, had gotten the doll house she'd wanted as a gift, and now her backyard has several puddles from the rain that's just fallen. Her mom had insisted on her wearing boots and sits on the porch, drinking coffee and keeping watch.

In a different place, Mabel walks along the street, rolling her eyes at the group catcalling her and clutching the handle of her bag as they stalk her. With her newly done nails, she puts up a struggle when they try to viciously grab her.

In a small, dank room, a drunk man takes another swig at a bottle of vodka. The room's a mess, he hasn't taken the trash out in weeks, and there are bottles of vodka everywhere. His hair's a mess, and he's been wearing the same clothes for weeks—he just throws on a jacket when he has to go to the liquor store. Tears stream down his face as he drinks; a picture frame lies on the ground not far from his spot, shattered with the picture of a happy couple slipping out.

Under an elm tree at a park, Ben and Stacy embrace and kiss with fervent passion. It's their anniversary, just two years being officially together even though they've known each other since middle school. They grab at each other, hands in their hair, under their jackets, behind their necks, and whisper professions of love with breathless voices.

Tires screech on the main road as a white jeep tries to avoid hitting the back of a black Kia that's suddenly stopped, but there's an alarming crash, and the jeep swerves into a different car. It's several minutes before the ambulance gets there,

In the realm of light where Paul and the seraph are watching everything, Caviel gives a simple nod to Paul.

Paul has never been to the mortal realm. He is a soul that has known not life and death. The world he sees is good but bad, filled with a light that's dying and a darkness that's spreading.

Another angel, a cherub, makes an entrance, interrupting Caviel and Paul. Cherubs are beings of perfect appearance, this one especially with stars adorning her body and wonderous fire on her head. Her skin is snow and her flowing gown gold. Cheviel hovers barefoot, representing not just beauty but integrity—a gentle

12

beckoning. She looks to both Caviel and Paul, glancing only once at the mortal realm.

Caviel shakes his head; cherubs are the most dramatic of their world, Cheviel more than most.

"What?" Cheviel asks.

"Must you always make such blinding entrances?!"

She smiles at him. "I was made to shine as bright as the sun," and to Paul, she asks, "Are you ready?"

Paul has his attention back on the mortal realm, having recovered from Cheviel's theatrical appearance. "I don't know if I am." He looks up at her and asks, "How can I know?"

"You were chosen at this time because you are ready, Paul," Caviel says. "You were chosen, that's how you know.".

"But many were chosen as well, and they failed. What if I lose myself? What if I can't find the way home?"

"Have you spoken with Father?" Cheviel asks.

"I have. I chose a difficult path…to honor Him."

"It's not going to be easy; there is no memory of this eternity; it's why they lose their way."

Paul is unsettled now. The light of his form flickers as he gazes on the earth intensely. Caviel stands a bit closer to him.

"You won't be without your gifts, Paul. Take comfort in that."

"Yes, that should help," Cheviel adds, "You will touch many lives, but in order to do so, you will need to overcome yourself, your humanity, your weakness, and your demons."

Paul inhales deeply. Caviel sighs as well and watches him. He has not moved or spoken. The realm of light is filled with whispers because its inhabitants love to talk or sing or do anything other than stand still and quiet. It worries the seraph how Paul's light has settled to be a bit less bright.

Still, Paul is silent.

Both angels hear something inaudible to Paul and turn their heads towards it in unison. "It is time," Cheviel says solemnly. It's a sad thing that she cannot find something comforting to say to him.

Now, he must follow her to where he will be taken to the mortal world and be born.

"Perhaps," he says as Cheviel turns, speaking to Caviel. "Perhaps if I lose my way and cannot seem to find it…perhaps you might guide me."

Caviel attempts to speak, but Cheviel cuts him. "He cannot…unless Father permits him, which might not happen if you do not ask it of Him in prayer. Do not forget that Father's gift to them is free will, there will be no interruptions from any of us. No matter how much it hurts us to watch." The last sentence is barely audible.

Caviel has nothing else to offer but a smile and a kind farewell before Paul follows Cheviel. They walk away from the realm of light and all its splendor, and soon the hubbub fades into perfect silence. No whispers, no songs, no circle of perfect cherubs dancing and laughing. It makes Paul's light dim further.

"Your connection to here won't be fully untethered. It's the reason you'll still have your gifts; your link to your eternal self won't be severed completely. Consider that a gift."

She stops and steps aside, gesturing for Paul to continue the rest of the way. It's a long winding road, with the surreal dimness of the mortal world waiting at its end.

"I say that, but you must know that nothing in that world will be familiar."

Paul sets on the path to mortality, alone, excited and unsure. The only thing guiding him besides the sharpness of the road is the echo of Cheviel's voice.

*"…nothing in that world will be familiar…"*

Clare, a young woman curled into herself, sits in a corner. She's trembling and crying, half-naked in the dirty, dank room. The clothes on her back are ripped, a thrifted dress she'd been excited to find for its bargain price. Pieces of it are on the floor, mixed in drying blood.

The man, standing over her, swaying with the effects of alcohol—maybe drugs—grunts as he zips up. The rank smell of his cheap cigarette wafts about the room, and he leaves after flinging some dollar bills and an insult at her.

Neither of them sees it; the small light illuminating from inside Clare's womb. It'll be a few more weeks before she notices anything, a few more months before she swallows her fears and does a test. It's not her fault; nobody wants to remember a nightmare.

# Chapter
## ONE

It is raining. The sky is overcast with dark clouds that have plunged the world into a dull, wet depression. The wind is chilly and bites as it razes through streets and alleys, buildings and cars, carrying its cold howling rage through parks and their dying trees.

The earth is sick, it says, and the people—the pollution they have brought, and their neglect for what it does—are its sickness.

Cars blare their horns furiously, their drivers agitated and hollering obscenities at one another through their windows. Traffic is at a standstill in the Minnesota capital, and the torrential downpour is causing jaywalkers to run and pedestrians to flee to close-by stores for cover.

Women snatch up their toddlers and sprint for buses. Tires screech past a puddle and splash dirty water on a vagrant lying motionless on the sidewalk. He startles awake into a coughing sprint while the driver jeers at him.

"Loser!"

Some people, bored with the traffic and the rain, snicker and whisper while he tries to recover his lungs. He pushes himself off the cement, soaked through with the dirty, cold water, his tattered clothes clinging to him. The store glass behind him is warm to touch, but the owner comes out almost as soon as his hands touch it and threatens him with a broom to move.

The attempt to flee fails almost immediately as he falls to the ground, but somebody catches him when he tries to stand again, helping to steady him. For a moment, rain isn't splattering on his back.

"Are you all right?" When Paul looks up into the concerned face of a young man. He's holding up an umbrella with one hand, while the other is helping to hold Paul up.

Suddenly, because that is how these things come to him, Paul is overcome by a vision. One of those disorienting ones he'd been having since he was a kid, they take him to a place he's becoming familiar with, vast and bright and beautiful.

*He is translucent, like smoke but bright, and walking in a vast garden of flowers. Walking beside Him is somebody he cannot truly describe. The person—the being—is majestic, clothed in glory, sashed around the chest in wonders. His hair is snow, wool, cotton. When He speaks, His voice is like a song; perfectly harmonious.*

*"The world," He says, "is a beautiful place. A wondrous place filled with wonderous things and beautiful people…if you learn how to see it."*

*Paul is awestruck as he always is, conflicted in his heart between the turmoil in him and the effect of the garden, of this person. "What do I look for?" he asks softly. "The light. The divine spark that lies inside every human being. Cultivate that spark, help it grow and blossom like these flowers, and they find their way home. Extinguish it, and they are lost forever."*

*Paul stops walking. It's always the same with the visions. Always the same with dreams. It's like being given an equation you have no idea how to solve. "How do I...how do I avoid extinguishing the spark?"*

*This person, whom Paul slowly realizes to be the Son of God, stops before him and stares down at him with furiously bright eyes. "You will meet many people as you walk out that reality. Indeed, some of them are just for a moment, others for longer, but each of them significant. They will all, in their ways, by their actions and even inactions, add to your journey, and you do not want to miss that. Even if you lose your way, if you pay attention to them, the signs, no matter how small, will point you home."*

*The Son of God starts to fade. The vision is over, and Paul must leave, but before he goes, he is suddenly before a bridge overlooking a pasture. A stranger is on the other side, coming towards him.*

*"That is Bradley,"* the invisible being says with His voice that inspires reverence as the garden begins to fade as well, *"he wanted to meet you before you left."*

19

Because of that, Paul recognizes the man holding him up.

"Are you all right? How long have you been here? I think you just blacked out. Are you anemic? Are you hungry?"

Paul frowns at him, he wants to shake him off and leave, but he's cold and knows that he'll just stumble around for a bit before falling to the ground again.

"Yes," he says instead, "some food would be nice."

Gently, Bradley begins to lead them away, down the street cramped with umbrella wielders and people trying to outrun the wetness. "Oh, I'm Bradley, by the way."

Paul grunts and nods; he doesn't particularly feel like saying he already knew. "Paul."

"Yeah…I think I've seen you at the shelter."

"What shelter?" It's hard to walk, his joints are cold and creaking. Maybe sleeping against that store's glass had been a worse idea than he'd thought.

"There's only one shelter on this side of town. Well, it's more like a church that's a shelter, really, or maybe a shelter that's also a church? Not sure which it is, but I like the concept. It's cool, very out of the box."

"Oh right. I know that place." Paul glances at Bradley while they pass a car that's hit the backlights of the car in front of it. A small crowd is gathering around the commotion. He pauses while they navigate through the group and then continues. "I've only been there once, though. The food was horrible."

Bradley laughs. "Well, I volunteer there from time to time; they have a new cook. In fact, it's exactly where we're going right now." Paul groans. "Come on, the food's better, I think. We've got to get you there quick if you want to get some lunch, besides...they've got rooms and beds, more comfortable than being outside in the rain, I assure you. And they have a shower...which you need to take..."

# Chapter
## TWO

John gasps awake on the couch of his living room. There are dark circles under his eyes. Panting and sweating, he washes his hands over his face. The dream felt so real he could have touched it.

Around him is a mess. There are clothes draped all over the couch, a small pile of them nestled on one end of the couch. Water bottles and used plates are scrambled about, on the floor, on the end tables, the coffee table. In one corner, a bottle rolls away, and something small and loud scuttles under a chair. On the coffee table is a small patch clear of debris; on that patch is a laptop, a Bible, a notebook, and a small trinket of praying hands. John dives into the mess on the couch, searching for his phone to quickly write the little he remembers from his vivid dream.

*Save Paul...?* He sends it as a text to himself before trying to calm down.

He barely notices the time on his phone before Grace walks in and goes to the kitchen. Her dark clothes, the style he'd noticed she seemed to prefer more and more, fits her. Plenty of black with skulls and dragons printed on them.

He can't recall the last time he saw her wearing bright colors, though there was a picture of her on his laptop wearing a pretty yellow dress and smiling.

Grace doesn't crack a smile as she tosses snacks from the fridge and cabinet into her messenger bag.

"Good morning, Grace," John tries with a smile, trying not to allow his face to fall when she doesn't so much as glance at him. At least, she rolls her eyes as she walks past him to the front door. Acknowledgment. He could work with that.

"Have a good day, honey—" he says right before she shuts the door. With a bang.

The smile drops from his face after the bang, and he sighs before pulling himself up from the couch, stretching, and walking towards the front door.

Lily is coming down the stairs just then, neatly dressed in a business suit with her hair up. She's watching him wearily.

The smile forces its way in, heavier than before. "Good morning, Lily."

"John." The downturn of her lips deepens as she looks him over. Her scrutinizing eyes make him aware of how messy he looks. She hisses as she passes through the living room to pour herself some coffee.

"I—I had another dream last night," John begins as she takes her cup and heads for the front door. "It was very vivid this time, even though—" The door cuts him off with a slam.

Lily's gone too.

He sighs at the closed door. "…I thought, maybe, you would want to hear about it…"

When he goes to the window, he sees Lily sitting in her SUV, just holding on to the steering wheel and looking straight forward. She bends over the wheel, resting her forehead to it, her shoulders dropping. Then she swipes for something beside her and fidgets with it, her phone, maybe, before tossing it to the passenger's seat and looking back at the house.

Their eyes lock, and John waves and tries to smile again. It's a formed habit he doesn't have the strength to break. Nothing about this situation would be fixed with a simple smile.

Lily drives away, and his phone chimes. It's an email from her. "Divorce—Latest Draft" the subject line reads. He takes a deep, slow breath before putting the phone down and picking up his notebook to sketch.

The sketch is of the man he'd dreamt about. He takes his notebook and Bible with him when he drives out. The car moves slowly along the sidewalk of the street, slow enough so he can compare the faces of random people on the street to the face in his sketch. Despite the growing traffic behind him, John doesn't speed up. He ignores the honks, keeps up his search, all the way to the fellowship.

It's late in the morning when he reaches Tselem Fellowship, the homeless shelter. The compound is busy; people are clustered around, walking in and out. Some people just leaning against the rickety old fence, staring at nothing, some lying on the grass. A group of ragged people in old unwashed clothes are being addressed by a staff member from the shelter. They're standing under the sign with the shelter's name and tagline. John looks at it and reads the words to himself even though he's known those words for a while now.

"...saving the world one soul at a time..."

After the car is parked, John tears out the sketch and folds it into his back pocket before getting off.

Some of the homeless people wave at him as they walk past, holding packages they'd collected from inside. When he smiles and waves, they smile and wave back, greeting him cheerfully.

John pushes his way into the shelter just as a man is pushing his way out. Transfixed, John stands at the doorway, his palm still pressed against the door, watching the man's face. The stranger, a homeless man, must have felt him staring because he glances back.

Something clicks in his head; the homeless man's face is strangely familiar. John walks after the man and grabs his shoulder to get his attention. "Excuse me, please wait..." His other hand scrambles with his back pocket for the sketch.

The stranger, a tall dark man in damp tattered clothes, barely looks at John before his eyes are glazed over as if reminiscing something. John uses it as his chance to properly unfold the paper and confirm what he'd suspected.

*Paul, translucent, is standing with a man. A being of warm light. It is an angel, Aviel. Together, they stand before a pillar of fire, but when Paul looks up at the pillar, he finds that it is in the figure of a man. A golden hue surrounds this man, seeming to be a being of its own. The man holds a double-edged sword in his hand, looking straight ahead into the distance as if ready for a battle.*

*"Is he mortal?" Paul asks.*

*"In his mortal body, he looks nothing like this," Aviel replies, "but this is who he really is."*

*There is power emanating from the flames, bravery, and authority. Awe and wonder strike Paul as he beholds the warrior.*

*"What is his name?"*

*Aviel answers, "His name is John."*

John matched the faces; this was the man. Paul. From his dream.

When Paul comes to, he catches sight of the sketch and gives John a look. "What do you want?" he asks.

John clears his throat and extends a hand. "Hi, I'm Pastor John Williams, I'm in charge here." Paul only glances down at the hand, doesn't take it. John puts the hand away and stuffs the paper back into his pocket. "Okay, well, you see, I would very much like to help you."

A raised brow. "With what?"

"With everything. Anything you need help with."

Paul considers him for a moment. "The food wasn't as bad as the last time I ate here. I'd say you've helped plenty..." He turns and starts to walk away, but John follows.

"Yes, but there are other things I could help you with," he says as Paul walks on.

"I'm not interested."

John continues to follow. Paul stops walking abruptly and faces John. "No disrespect, sir, but the only things I need are a place to sleep and food to eat. I'm not interested in anything else."

"I can help you with those." John quickly says to keep Paul from leaving. "I can get you a good place to sleep, to rest your head. You wouldn't need to spend the night on the street."

Paul's eyes narrow slightly. "Why?"

"Huh?"

"Why do you want to help me so badly?"

"Oh." John laughs. "It's nothing really, I'm just trying my best to be obedient to the One I serve."

Paul stares at him, the expression on his face isn't easy to interpret, but his brown eyes are clear and piercing. John reacts instinctively with a wry smile because the thought of being seen through by anyone embarrasses him slightly. He's confident with his worries only when he prays. "...and that paper?"

"Oh." John pulls the crumpled paper out again and tries to straighten it. "Ah, I have dreams sometimes," he starts to explain, sure the reaction of Paul—whom he was beginning to see was a bit of a skeptic—would be somewhat similar to how Lily had reacted in the morning, but Paul's brows rise the slight bit, and his eyes widen a fraction. No doubt, just surprise.

But he recovers quickly, and the brow rises again. "Dreams?"

"Yes. Well, dreams, visions, anything you might want to call it, but I've seen you in them before. Several times, actually. It was only today that the image of your face actually stayed with me after I woke up. I understand so far, that I'm supposed to help you."

"Help me with what?"

For a moment, John's struck dumb. It's an answer he knows, he's known it every day for quite some time now, but at this moment, nothing comes to mind. Stuffing the sketch back into his back pocket, he smiles. "Well, a bed and some food for a start."

Paul considers this. He's barefoot, smells terrible, has patches in his clothes, and is in severe need of a comb and a visit to a barber, but he considers John and the offer so thoughtfully he didn't seem like a homeless person in need of basic amenities.

"I'll take you up on that offer, then," he says finally, "but on one condition."

John's smile widens. This was a peculiar man, all right. "What condition?"

"Don't preach to me."

John stifles a laugh. "Fair enough," he says, "I'm not really that kind of pastor anyway."

"Sure…" Paul scoffs.

# THREE

The iron bunks are brown with rust; the bed has a smell that's diluted by the clean bedsheet. The room is rowdy, men milling about, talking, eating, trading things in pseudo-secrecy. The light isn't too harsh, and the mash of people trying to find spaces to sleep for the night makes the room warmer despite the chill outside. It hasn't rained since earlier in the morning, but the grey solemnity has hung in the sky since, constantly threatening to bring the rain back.

Paul is sitting on the lower bed of the bunk, his head still reeling from the vision he'd had that day.

"Guess we're neighbors for the night, eh?" a handicapped man says, sitting in a wheelchair at the head of the next bunk. He doesn't have legs.

Paul shrugs off his coat and is reminded of Bradley before he lays it on the bed and lies on top of it. "Yeah, you and the other hundred guys here."

The man laughs. "True! I'm McAllister McKinney, by the way, but you can just call me Mac."

"Paul."

Mac wheels himself closer and extends a hand. Paul hesitates but takes the hand.

*Mac, younger, with an orange glow emanating from his skin, is running through an open field. It's bright and loud; he's panting, sweating, and children are chasing after him.*

Quickly, Paul takes his hand back and only manages to not wipe it on his pants.

"You okay, buddy?" Mac asks with furrowed brows.

"Yeah, I'm fine." Paul's breathing is a bit too hard; his chest is rising and falling too quickly.

Mac purses his lips. "You sure? You look like you spaced out for a moment there, buddy…"

The legs of Mac's pants are tied in knots less than a foot away from his waistband.

"In case you're wondering—" Paul looks away, focusing on the top bunk.

"I'm not."

"—I was born this way. People always wonder, so I prefer to let it out early. Sorry to disappoint, but there's no war story, no horrific accident, nothing. Just good old luck. I've been living like this my whole life…"

Paul sighs and turns away, lying on his side. "Congratulations."

Mac laughs. "Man! I like you, Paul. You're a hoot."

"Even hoots need to sleep, Mac. Good night."

"All right, fine. I know I run my mouth like water sometimes, so I'll turn the faucet off. Good night, neighbor."

The wheels move back, and the bed behind Paul rustles. Mac grunts as he pulls himself on the bed.

"Good night, Paul," he says again just as a volunteer comes in to shout "lights out" and plunge most of the hall into darkness. A few people have cell phones out, and the dim lights illuminate their distant faces as Paul drifts to sleep with joint aching from another day of being alive.

*Paul opens his eyes to find himself high above the ground, high above everything. Somehow, the whole world is visible from where he's standing. Somebody is standing beside him, a beautiful man with a kind smile and warm bright light filtering out of him. It is the angel, Caviel.*

*"It is time," he says, staring right at Paul.*

*Paul looks down at the world. It's darker than the sleeping hall after the light was put out, and the darkness seems to be moving, swallowing, and plunging more of the world into its abyss.*

*Caviel is speaking again. "Poor choices can lead to a cataclysmic chain of events. It can destroy cities, nations, even the world."*

*The darkness swallows everything. Everything. The world is an endless stretch of perfect darkness.*

*Paul swallows. This is too much. "I'm just one man..."*
*he whispers. This is too much for him.*
*Caviel smiles. "One has always been enough."*
*"What do you want from me? Why won't you leave me*
*alone?!"*
*"You need to find yourself, Paul. A spark is all a forest*
*needs to burn, and you are the spark that was sent. You*
*stand apart from Him, from our Father, and contribute to*
*the darkness there. You must find yourself to ignite the*
*forest."*
*Paul shakes his head. "No. No, I can't do that. I don't*
*understand what you're saying, but I can't do it. Whatever*
*you're expecting of me, stop it. You don't know what I've*
*been through. You don't know what I've done."*
*Caviel is watching Paul, with brilliant heavy eyes. The*
*compassion in them forces Paul to look away. "Allow me*
*to show you something..." he says and gently presses a*
*hand to Paul's chest.*
*He shows Paul utter chaos. Cities set alight, hoards of*
*people fleeing on foot, on bikes, in cars, people fighting on*
*the streets, hitting, breaking, smashing. Insanity reigns,*
*people pull out their hair, mutter to themselves, cut their*
*skin, their eyes ignited with rage. Somewhere in the chaos,*
*Paul is standing, watching, weeping.*
*"I know it is not easy; I know what you have suffered,*
*Paul."*
*A tear slides down Paul's cheek. His chest is still warm*
*with the heat of the chaotic world.*

*"How would you know?"*

*"There are no secrets under the sun. Stop running. It is not in your nature to flee."*

Paul jolts awake, shivering in a cold sweat. It's morning, and the chill air has seeped into the hall. Even though he's shivering, there's an odd, warm sensation burrowing inside his chest.

*...allow me to show you something...*

"Are you okay, man?" Mac calls.

"Yeah…" Paul shakes himself, shakes off the strange feeling of his dream—nightmare? "Yeah…I'm okay…"

"You sure? You're shaking pretty hard."

"I'm fine. I just…I need to talk to John."

"The Pastor? He's usually in his office around this time, but it's a Saturday, so he's probably home. The secretary is probably here though. She's always here."

Chapter
# FOUR

The ringing phone carries along with the silence of the house. John's laying on the couch. It has been cleaned up, and he's bundled in cover cloth as if he's going to sleep, staring at the ceiling in thought. It takes a while for the ringing to snap him out of his thoughts.

It's Cher. "Good morning, Pastor. There's a Paul Samson here waiting to see you. He says he might be needing help with more than just food and a bed…or something like that. Apparently, you'd understand what he means."

John burst into a smile. "Great! I'll be there soon. Please tell him."

He smiles at his phone for a short while. Such good news, he's very happy, very excited.

"Off to save somebody else, I see," Lily says, entering the living room. Her voice startles John. He hadn't heard her come down.

He gets up awkwardly. "Lily. Good morning. I didn't realize you were off today…"

Her face drops into a frown. "The heck, John, it's Saturday! I haven't worked on a Saturday in nearly ten years, and you didn't even realize. Freaking perfect." She throws her hands up. "Typical!"

John grimaces at himself and doesn't follow her into the kitchen. Somehow, he keeps making things worse.

"…I have to go by the office," he tries, "but I should be back in a couple of hours. I won't be there all day."

Lily moves about the kitchen, preparing to cook something. She ignores him though she's still frowning and looking frustrated.

"I won't stay the whole day, I promise." He grabs his keys, pockets his phone, and heads out. He doesn't see Lily slam the refrigerator door and bang her forehead against it.

Paul is in the waiting room, seated and leaning forward on his knees. He's picking at his nails, glancing at Cher every so often as she works.

He glances at John as he approaches and stands up. "Hi, again…*Pastor* John…"

"Hi Paul, just John will do. No need for awkwardness. Miss Ames, good morning, no calls or visitors, please. I'm pretty much not here."

Cher nods at him with a smirk on her face.

"Nice meeting you, Cher." Paul manages as John begins to lead him away.

"It's Miss Ames to you, *sir*…" she frowns at him before he enters John's office. Cher never takes warmly to newcomers at first; it's a habit John's learned to overlook since she's a good person and a great secretary.

He catches Paul staring at the cross on his desk as he locks the door and goes around to sit behind the desk. He pauses instead of sitting. "Are you doing okay?" he asks after Paul looks away from the cross to his hands with a heavy sigh.

"Yeah, I'm great. I don't think your secretary wants me here though."

John scuffs and takes his seat. "Why wouldn't she want a homeless person in a homeless shelter? She's just…particular. You're a new face around here. She'll be cold at the beginning, she's always like that, but once you get to know her, she warms up. All warmed up, Cher will be one of the best people you'll ever meet."

The wind blows through the open window and flusters the documents on John's desk. One of the papers flies off, but Paul catches it. John opens his mouth to thank him, but his mouth hangs open.

"Paul?" He gets up and rushes around the table to catch Paul before he hits the ground. "Paul!"

*Paul sees John standing before two roads. One is made of solid gold, littered with diamonds, and bordered by dainty, blooming flowers that curve upwards gently. The road runs far into the distance, disappearing down a gentle hill. Overhead, the sky is cloudless and sunny. An angel is standing next to the road of gold.*

*The other road is unpaved. Creeping along its sides to mark its borders are withered, thorny vines. The road stretches into the distance like a wound and disappears into a red, angry glow. Overhead, the sky is grey and dim, with thick dark moving clouds that allow a crimson moon to peek through. A demon—a being with leathery wings and blood-red skin, with horns sprouted crookedly on its head—stands by the road and smiles when he catches John's eyes. He motions for John to come to him, his forked tongue flicking out of his smiling mouth.*

*When John stakes for the golden road, the demon gnarls while the angel smiles. When he dodges for the scarred road, the demon grins while the angel's face falls.*

*As Paul stares at it, the road behind the demon darkens. Muffled screams come through, shouts of pain, agony, torture.*

John slaps Paul's face slightly, but he won't come to. He's shaking, trembling, while John tries to wake him up.

Cher comes in, gasps, and rushes to John's side. "Is he all right? What's happening?"

"I don't know. There, take that paper from him."

Cher takes the paper, worry etched into her face. "Sh— should I call an ambulance?" Just then, Paul stops shaking. His breathing is rapid but calming down, though his eyes are still closed.

"I'm fine," Paul manages to say a little above a whisper.

"Miss Ames, I think he's fine. Don't worry about it. Go back to your desk, okay?"

Cher leaves reluctantly, just as John shakes Paul to come back to himself. Paul opens his eyes slowly.

"Hey, man, what happened? You look like you were having a seizure…"

Paul sits up in John's grip and glances around the office. "I'm fine…" He gets up, gaining his strength.

John hesitates a little but gets up too and goes back behind the desk to sit.

"I can see…" Paul says immediately. John settles down.

Quickly, John glances around his desk but doesn't see anything that stands out. "…that's…good to know…"

"No. I mean, I can really see. Well, when I'm not drunk at least. I can see…the world beyond."

John scrambles his brows for a moment. There's silence, and Paul visibly winces at what he's just said.

"Do you mean…like a seer, Paul?" John asks finally.

He shrugs. "I guess? Apparently, there is this thing or the other I need to do. I keep getting these visions whenever I…touch things…or people. It's very disorienting. If I weren't so poor, I'd be walking up and down with gloves. He said I was sent here or agreed to come here or something like that, that I need to stop running away from what I needed to do."

"Agreed to come here? As if you existed before being born?"

He shrugs again, leans back into the chair, and nods at the Bible at the corner of the desk sitting above a pile of documents. "I thought it said somewhere there that God knew us even before we were formed in the womb."

"Yes, but I've always taken that to have some sort of deep metaphorical meaning."

"I don't know. Apparently, there's nothing impossible for God. I don't think He needs metaphors for things like this. I think we all existed in His mind or something before coming here. We were definitely somewhere. That's for sure. Something like whatever is in His mind is already in existence, waiting to be made manifest into being or in creation."

"I—I'm not following…" John says, giving Paul a small, confused smile.

"I mean, if we come into this world, we must have existed somewhere before. That somewhere must have been God's mind, where we all exist; where we all come from."

"Sounds like universalism to me. Like, there is this one universal mind, consciousness or whatever."

"Everything in this room was first a thought in a man's mind. Was it only real when it became something we can see and touch, or was it real at its conception?"

Slowly, John nods his head. "So, you're saying that every human being was first in God's mind before being born here?"

"Yeah. You get it. Why do you think we need to be born again here? When it's not as if we can repeat our physical birth..."

John takes in what he's hearing slowly, leans back into his chair, and releases a breath. It's a lot to digest, and he's without his notebook. "That's a lot to digest," he points out. "A whole lot."

"I'm not sure exactly what I'm here to do, but I need to make the change starting now. I want to start helping people."

Paul's lips are set in determination. John sits up. It's always great seeing people reach this conclusion by themselves. "There are many people who need help. That's good."

"There's something I need to do first," he adds. "I would like to be baptized."

John takes a while to register it, just a few seconds, but then he gives Paul a small smile even though it's obvious how pleased he is with the announcement. He grabs his key, and together, they head out.

John brings Paul to a pool that he often uses for baptisms. He gives Paul a long look as if he's expecting Paul to change his mind, but then Paul motions for him to lead the way.

A short while later, they are both standing in the pool, and John solemnly asks, "Paul, do you renounce the world and choose to walk with God; accept His Son, Jesus Christ as your Master and Saviour?"

"Yes."

John holds Paul's hands to his chest and pushes him gently into the pool. Paul goes down, for a while.

*When he goes into the water, time slows down. The environment changes, broadens, loses its boundaries and extends all the way into the realm of light.*

*From the being of God, a bright spark ignites and takes form. It begins to look like a foetus, a little bright light curled inside a greater light. This baby of light descends through time and space, through the matrix of all creation, from the being of God, all the way down to the point on the earth where Paul is immersed in water. The baby of light hits Paul's body as he is pulled out of the pool, erupting into blue flames that spread over his body, burning but not consuming.*

*When John holds Paul out of the pool, he is a burning inferno of blue flames.*

"Come, Holy Spirit." John says, holding Paul. He notices Paul's eyes, for the ghost of a moment, he sees them burn a bright blue light before fading back to their normal brown color.

"Did you see that?" Paul asks.

"See what?"

He purses his lips and shakes his head at John. "You really should learn to see properly, John."

"Fair enough, but what would I have seen?" Together, they drudge their way out of the pool. Cher's holding a towel with a worried look. She hasn't said a word, but she's been watching Paul as if she expects him to fall to the ground at any moment.

"The birth of a new creation," Paul says with a smile.

After John's clothes dry and Paul's given a new set of clothes, they head out, driving down the street, still discussing. There's much to talk about. Paul's sitting in the passenger's seat, watching people go about their day. "It's funny," he begins, "how we go about our daily lives without knowing that there is this vast, infinite, yet unseen world that is superimposed over this one, extending beyond time."

John clears his throat. "How do we help them?"

"You already know the answer, John. You change the world one soul at a time; like your tagline says."

"There are almost eight billion people on the planet, just so you know..."

"Yeah...makes you wonder how much difference one man can make, yet here we are. We save one and have no idea how we've changed the lives of possibly a thousand people."

"...like the domino effect?"

"Something like that, yes."

"I've been thinking about giving you a job at the shelter, just to help you get on your feet...I don't know just what you can do just yet..."

"That's fine. I used to be an accountant...some years ago."

A smile extends on John's face, and he drums on the steering wheel a bit. "Perfect. We usually contract that department of the shelter out to freelancers. The salary might be sub-standard though."

"That's fine. I've been unemployed for a while. I might as well be doing something. Thank you, I appreciate it."

"I'm also curious about your story. You really don't behave like the type who usually ends up on the street...how'd you get there? If you don't mind my asking."

"I don't mind it, but my story isn't anything worth telling. Not right now, anyway."

They drag to a stop at a red light, and across the road, a posh car pulls up to the curb of an apartment building. An elegant, middle-aged woman steps out from the car and into the building, escorted by a buff bodyguard. John notices Paul watching her.

"That's Melinda Martinez," he says before Paul asks. "...she owns these streets. I'm sure she's responsible for some of the violence and corruption that goes on in this city. Drug deals, organized crime, illegal shipments. She's got a tight hand in them, but she apparently also has a heart. Several times now, she's tried to give our church money. We refuse her, but I guess that's just her humanitarian side."

Melinda and her bodyguard make their way down a large passageway towards a door at the other end of it. They enter and meet a man in his sixties, plump, serious-looking, and smoking a cigar. The man shakes her hand and offers her a seat. The bodyguards shut the door.

The traffic light turns green, Paul and John start to move again.

"She takes care of people, though sometimes not with the most righteous ways, sometimes, even employing just chaos. We've, however, had some measure of peace for a while now, though things like that are usually short-lived in this world."

"So," Paul speaks after a while. "she's like a stronghold?"

"Something like that, I suppose. I've been having some troublesome dreams lately. The city is in chaos; it's on fire. Sometimes, I even see you standing untouched in the midst of it all." John laughs. "The first few times, I thought you were the villain I was supposed to look out for. Anyways, I can tell something is coming…I can sense it. I just don't know what it is or how to prevent it.

"One soul at a time, John!" Paul emphasizes exasperatedly. John glances between Paul and the road, wearing a confused expression.

Paul breaths slowly for a while before speaking again. "I need you to help me with something."

Cher's already back at the shelter by the time John drives in. She's just finishing a call as he and Paul head back for his office. "Sir," she calls to him, "Miss Martinez just called. She's coming to see you."

His mouth is in a thin line. What he'd agreed to help Paul with just doesn't sit well with him. There are so many ways it could go wrong; just thinking about it almost makes him stagger. But he forces a smile. "Great. Send her in when she comes."

Cher's brows rise in surprise. It's the first time he has decided to speak with Melinda since all the attempts the woman had made to donate money to them. Usually, he'd avoid it by saying he was out of office at the moment. "Are you sure? Have you forgotten the kind of person she is?"

John purses his lips and shakes his head. "No, Miss Ames, I still remember."

"I hope you know what you're doing." She says with a sigh and picks up the phone to relay the message.

The hope was mutual; he hoped he knew what he was doing as well.

"This is a terrible idea," John says, fidgeting with his hands on the desk. "I can feel it."

Paul is standing behind him, perched on the windowsill, peeking through the curtain. "I just need to get close enough to touch her. How can that be dangerous?"

"Did you not hear any of the things I said on our drive? No. No, this is definitely a bad idea, I'm telling you."

Paul smiles at the window. "I heard you the first three hundred times," he mutters.

When Melinda's posh car pulls up at the shelter, there is a heavily tinted car parked across the street. The driver's window is halfway down, and Brett Edwards, a middle-aged detective, removes his sunglasses. His eyes are hard, determined, as he watches Melinda enter the building. With furrowed brows, he pulls out a notepad onto his lap and started to jot down something. His prosthetic hand rests easy beside him.

# FIVE

Lily tries to focus and read through the most recent copy of the divorce papers, but her eyes are watery. She's been trying to blink them away, but they refuse to leave.

Grace comes to her side and hugs her. "It's going to be okay, Mom."

"I don't know. I can't do this; I shouldn't be doing this. It feels so wrong…"

"What difference does it make? He's almost never home anyway."

"Maybe if I gave him a little more support…I mean, shouldn't I be his helpmate? A partner? Instead of pursuing my own dreams and career?"

"Mom! For goodness' sake, he doesn't even care. Dad cares more about saving the world than saving his own family."

"How have we made that a bad thing?"

Grace sighs and pulls away. "I need to go. Do you need anything?"

Sniffling, Lily dabs her eyes with the back of her hands, tucks the papers into an envelope, and hands it to grace. "Help me drop this at your father's office, please."

Grace rolls her eyes but takes the envelope. "Is there anything else you want?"

Back at John's office, somebody knocks on the door, and John shoots up, his nerves fraying. He clears his throat and tries to mimic Paul's calm. "Come in."

Melinda enters with a smile. Her bodyguard stays close to the door after he shuts it. "John, lovely to meet you again. It's been so long." She shakes his hand. "I take it you've finally come to your senses."

"Hardly."

"And who's this?" Melinda asks, her sharp eyes on Paul.

"This is Paul. He works here…"

Paul gets up with a smile and offers his hand. She doesn't take it. It would have been easier if she did.

Paul glances at the bodyguard. He knows what he needs to do. What he doesn't know is if he will live to tell about it. Paul grabs Melinda's wrist.

*A translucent woman, with glorified features that loosely resemble Melinda, hovers high above the world, looking down at everything. She's watching the darkness seeping across the face of the earth.*

*A majestic angel floats alongside her. "Can we truly remedy the darkness as mortals?" the translucent Melinda asks.*

*"Every human being born into the earth either adds to its light or adds to its darkness…"*

Paul snaps back to reality with a gun aimed at his head. The bodyguard is tense, finger on the trigger. John has a hand up, trying to maintain calm. Melinda snatches her hand back and clutches it absent-mindedly.

"Please don't shoot. He's not trying to harm you."

She motions for the bodyguard to lower his gun and asks, glancing between Paul and John, confused, "John, what's going on here? Why did you decide to meet me?"

"I know that you want to help the people of this city, Melinda, but how you're doing it—the drugs and guns—is a disaster waiting to happen."

"I've seen you struggle with this place, struggling to get funding because you refuse to accept what I'm offering. You struggle in ways I don't; my business provides for this city."

"We had four overdose cases last week. Four different traumatized families that we had to take care of—two children now orphaned."

Melinda scoffs. "You can't measure success by minor failures."

"There's another way," Paul interjects before John can reply. Melinda's eyes snap to him.

"How would you know?"

"Every human born into the earth," Paul says carefully, "either adds to the light or adds to the darkness."

Melinda blinks at him. For a breath, her face is perfectly blank, then her brows furrow. She frowns and glares at both men before stomping away, her bodyguard in tow.

"What just happened?" John asks, looking at the door with a confused face. Paul doesn't reply; he's lost in thought, looking at nothing when Grace bursts through the door.

Both men jump while Cher comes in behind her, an apologetic look on her face.

"I tried to stop her, sir…" she starts to say but is cut off when John holds up a hand.

"It's fine."

Cher nods and leaves after casting Grace a look. After the door closes, Grace walks past John and Paul and slams the envelope on the desk, pulling out a pen from the cup on the table and slamming it down as well. John picks up the envelope, sighs at the bold address scribbled across it. *Able Law Firm*, and hesitates before opening it.

Paul is confused. The tension in the room has skyrocketed, and he looks from John to Grace, worried. When Grace's eyes meet his, Paul is sucked into a vision.

*It's a bedroom. Grace's bedroom. The window is closed and almost completely covered by the blinds. The bedside light is on, and it casts a faint glow across the room, drawing long shadows. The closet door hags open, and dark clothes hang on half-heartedly to hangers, some of them crumpled on the carpet. Grace is on her bed, unconscious. Her head is tilted to the side, and her arms are flung out. In one hand, there's an empty prescription bottle.*

*She isn't breathing...*

Paul shakes the vision away, not making sense of anything. Up until now, he was only able to have visions about people when they touched him in any way. It's never happened like this before; without physical contact.

John clears his throat. "Paul," he calls and gestures, "This is Grace, my daughter. Grace, this is Paul."

Grace doesn't so much as blink Paul's way. She's glaring at John, arms crossed with a foot slowly tapping against the wooden floor. It's as if Paul isn't even there.

"I'm just here for your signature, *sir*; I don't want to meet your friends."

She isn't leaning on anything, just standing close to the table, watching John with harsh eyes. She's swaying slightly on her feet, ever so slightly, and her nails are digging into her arms, scraping slowly, as if trying to scratch an itch without anybody else noticing. Paul observes quietly.

The papers are taken out of the envelope and signed. Grace snatches them before John can put them back properly and marches out of the office, slamming the door behind her.

Paul waits for a breath after she's gone, just feeling the tension lessen by folds. "Well…that seemed…intense…"

John lets out a breath and leans over his table. "Those were divorce papers," he says, "My wife is leaving me."

"Oh, I—I'm sorry." After a pause, Paul speaks again, "I noticed she…eh…I noticed Graced looked like some people I see on the streets, people who are—"

"Don't." John cuts him short with a hand. "Grace has had a hard time. My marriage has been like poison to her, and she has been drowning in it for half her life. Hopefully, having it all over and done with will help."

"John, I saw her—"

"How? How would you have seen anything? You didn't even touch her."

"I know, I can't explain it—"

"Then maybe what you saw wasn't real."

"I can help her John."

"There's enough people here that need help, Paul." John walks to the door and opens it for Paul. "Let's start with them."

*Mac is running through an open field; children are chasing after him. He is perfectly toned, with an orange glow emanating from his skin. He has legs.*

The place is crowded with men; deep voices and smells fill the air as Paul looks around. Mac is in a corner, talking to another man. Paul motions for John to follow him over.

"What are we doing?" John asks in a hushed tone as they navigate through the sea of homeless men.

"Helping People," Paul answers as he approaches Mac. "Hey Mac, I need to see your...where your legs should be."

"Paul, what are you doing?" John holds on to Paul's sleeve, trying not to wince at the statement.

Mac's companion frowns at him. "Yeah, man, don't be rude."

"No, you don't understand. I believe I can help you, Mac. I believe I can heal you."

Mac looks at him skeptically.

John firms his hold on the sleeve of Paul's shirt and hauls him away. "Hey, buddy, I can appreciate your boldness and tenacity, but we are not talking about high blood pressure or diabetes here. This is a case of missing legs, as in, there is nothing there where they should be. Never was, never can be."

"Maybe not in this realm. Do you believe, Pastor, that this physical world you see, this world we have created for ourselves, is the real world?"

"Obviously, the answer to that should be no, but..."

"Can you trust me? If it doesn't work, what have we to lose?"

"Nothing, I suppose, just our dignity. Maybe our pride as well, reputation, integrity…" John's counting off his fingers, Paul leaves him and goes back to Mac.

"Mac, please. Let me try. In the end, if it doesn't work, you're no worse off than you are now and you would have at least helped me to know if I can help people the way I think I'm supposed to. Please…"

Mac looks up at all of them. At Paul, at John, and at his surly friend. "Okay. Fine." He reaches for the ends of his pants and undoes the knots there, then he rolls back the pant legs to show two pale stumps of skin.

John's eyes dart everywhere, he's fidgeting too. But Paul calmly kneels beside Mac and closes his eyes. "By the authority I have in His Name, I command these legs to grow out and come in alignment with Mac's eternal reality right now."

Paul opens his eyes and joins the other men in holding his breath. It's an anxious and short while, but nothing happens.

Mac starts to say, "Well, there you—" but his words catch in his throat, and he suddenly begins to convulse and scream. Bones are tearing through his skin. Each bone grows, muscles coming outwards, veins, and skin following after. The convulsions throw Mac to the ground; he's crying as his new legs extend in front of him, presently forming heels touching the floor.

The crowd around hushed and watched, most of them as wide-eyes and speechless as John. When the ordeal is over, Mac gently pulls himself up from the ground, holding on to his wheelchair for support as he tries to stand. There's no pain in his newly formed bones to assure him that he isn't dreaming, his breath is coming fast and harsh, and as he's moving, he keeps looking up to Paul to be sure that he's still there; as if the spell of the dream would be undone if Paul leaves. He has never felt, seen, been able to use the rest of his legs. The tears in his eyes make his vision a bit blurry.

Cher bursts through the crowd, gawking at the sight of a standing Mac, even though he's wobbling like a fawn.

"Is—is this a dream?" his voice is faint as he asks through his tears. He losses his grip on the wheelchair and almost collapses to the ground, but John grabs him and supports him.

"Easy there, fellow. One step at a time."

# Chapter
## SIX

It's the start of something.

After Mac, Paul does many things in the following days. Weeks. They are driving down the street, and Paul motions for John to make a sharp turn. He's seen a hit and run in his visions. When they arrive, the police and EMTs are not yet there, and Paul lays his hand on the accident victim, who is able to get up after. They leave, but not before Brett's car pulls up the curb, and he sees Paul touch the woman to heal her. When he tries to go after them, the overjoyed victim calls him over and talks excitedly about what had just happened. Neither Paul nor John see Brett look down the street they'd driven down with narrowed eyes.

Paul, who had run away from the calling for so long, devotes time to reading the Bible on his bed. It took some getting used to, but every day, it gets easier.

When Paul escorts John to help with baptizing, there is a line of people waiting for them. It doesn't take long before the local newspapers begin to print about them. One of the headlines reads *False Prophet or the Real Deal?* The headlines make John shake his head, though he notices that the other headlines report declining crime rates and drug-related incidents in the city.

Melinda sits in her living room, her daughter asleep on her lap. She's watching the news about drug and gun-related crimes being down—watching the news reports about John and Paul going around healing, baptizing, and changing lives; she switches the television off.

Several People watch videos of Paul performing miracles on their phones. They show the videos around, sharing with social media group chats, helping the videos to gather attention. Paul has a vision, at another time, about an elderly woman having a heart attack after being mugged in a park. They arrive before Brett and Paul touches her. Brett is able to watch it happen, to see her get up. He tries to follow them, but the woman waves him over.

Paul has another vision about a shootout while he's cleaning the fellowship and rushes over without John. This time, Brett arrives at the same time and manages to stop Paul just as he lays his hands on one of the victims' chests.

"I can help him," Paul tries to argue.

But Brett counters firmly. "Unless you're a doctor or an EMT, you're not going anywhere near the victim." He doesn't understand what's happening, and he never trusts anything he doesn't understand. Whatever they were doing, he planned to get to the bottom of it.

John and Paul clean the pews and the floor; Paul is sweeping while John polishes the wooden seats. It's the next day after the shootout.

"He really stopped you from helping that victim?" John asks, wiping the cloth over the seats.

"We're not doing anything wrong, are we? If we were the ones who were hurting people, that would have been another matter, but we're saving lives. What's there to be suspicious about?"

"I know him. I've seen him before, sneaking around. There was a car outside my house a few days ago, and yesterday, he thought I didn't notice him peeking around the corner when I was coming in. He's set up camp by the side of the building. It's insane."

Paul stops sweeping. "Come to think of it, I thought I saw him walking behind me when I went for a walk today. I thought it was just my imagination, sensing something that wasn't really there."

John makes a face at him, so Paul quickly adds, "I mean like normal people imagining things…"

"Let's just keep an eye out. We don't want to ever be seen as visible suspects for anything." John reaches for the broom Paul is using, and as he takes it, their hands make contact, and Paul is sucked into a vision.

*It's Grace's room again. She's on the bed...again, stretched out with the empty pill bottle in one hand. Only that she isn't unconscious yet, she's trembling violently.*

Paul has a look of horror on his face. "Grace," he whispers.

"What? Wh—what happened? Did you see something?"

"Something's wrong. We need to go to her, now."

John drops everything and rushes for the exit with Paul right behind him.

Brett is outside, standing and rubbing his prosthetic hand. He and Paul lock eyes for a brief second before Paul jumps into the car with John and rushes down the street. Paul sees Brett enter his police cruiser and follow.

John's driving fast, throwing Paul worried glances every few seconds. His hands tremble visibly on the steering wheel, and every time he tries to say something, he just shakes his head and licks his lips and whispers to himself that everything's going to be fine. Paul doesn't speak a word through the drive; he just watches the rearview mirror and tries not to think about anything bad happening to Grace even though he knows better.

Grace's door is locked. John tries again, harsher, pounding the door and shouting for her. "Grace?! Open the door. Grace!"

When there's still no response, he backs up and crashes into the door with his shoulder, he hurts himself, but the pain doesn't overtake the worry and fear on his face.

Grace is exactly as Paul had seen her. On her bed, unconscious.

Paul goes to her and gently lays his hand on her while John paces behind him, phone in his hands. "Grace, wake up!"

Nothing happens.

"I don't have a signal," John says as he tries to dial again. When Paul looks up, he sees Grace's translucent body hanging above them, near the ceiling. He stares directly at Grace's soul.

"Grace, you need to get back in your body now."

Grace's soul doesn't acknowledge that he's speaking to her. She remains unmoved.

John freezes from his pacing. "What's wrong? Wake her up!"

Paul looks at him helplessly as Grace's soul ascends outside the room. "I'm trying, but nothing is working. She's leaving."

"What do you mean she's leaving? She's right there. Try harder. Right now."

Paul looks intently at Grace and holds her hand. "Grace, you need to wake up. Please…"

They both look at Grace, who is still unmoving. John begins to shake her and call her name, lightly slapping her and pulling apart her eyelids. "Grace, come on, please. Don't do this."

Paul lifts Grace in his arms. "Grab the bottle so they'll know what she took; we have to get her to the hospital."

Brett is standing on the front porch when they rush out of the house. "We need to get my daughter to the hospital!" John says as they rush by him to the car. After putting Grace in the back seat, John rushes into his car. Brett goes for his cruiser, and together, they drive to the hospital with Brett's sirens blaring.

The hospital is rowdy when Paul carries Grace in, a mix of the ailing and the healthy buzzing around.

John shouts frantically, "Help! We need some help over here."

An ER nurse rushes to them. "What happened?" she asks.

"We think she overdosed," John says, handing the nurse the empty bottle.

They put Grace on a gurney and start to check her vitals. "Are you the father?" she asks Paul, strapping Grace in and moving her towards an open bay.

"No," John answers, "I am. I've already called her mother too; she's on her way."

In the open bay, other nurses start hooking Grace to various machines. "She doesn't have a heartbeat," one of them reports.

"Blood pressure is dropping." Another nurse says.

The ER nurse touches Grace's skin, checking for a pulse. "Her pulse is weak..." When they bring in the defibrillator, she turns to John and Paul. "I need both of you to step away for a moment, please." They step back and the curtain is drawn. John stares at it, desperate and horrified.

The nurses cut Grace's shirt open. "Clear!" The defibrillator makes her body jolt, but the heart monitor doesn't pick up anything. They charge for another attempt.

"Clear!"

They try again with a higher voltage, and the jolt of Grace's body is sharper, but there's no other response. The heart monitor is still flat. Silent.

The ER nurse puts her arms down, breathing hard with a defeated look on her face. She shakes her head, and Paul barely catches John before he almost collapses on the floor.

He can see Grace's soul appearing, hovering close to her body.

"Again," Paul says to the nurse. "Just one more time, please."

The nurse looks at him for a short while before nodding. "Again."

John grips Paul's hand as the high whine of the machine charging is heard.

"Clear!"

He doesn't breathe as they press the defibrillator to Grace's chest. After the jolt, she doesn't stir. Silence rings in John's ear. The heart monitor is flat.

Paul watches the soul, Grace's soul, expand then contract. He watches it be accepted back into her body—the heart monitor beeps.

"We—we have a pulse…" the ER nurse announces quietly. The other nurses share small smiles, all of them relieved. John goes to the ground, kneels, then bends his forehead to touch the ground.

"Thank you, God." He says with a shaking voice.

"We're going to get her stabilized, then we'll let you know when you can come back and see her." The nurse hands over some forms on a clipboard from the admissions desk to Paul. "Please have him fill these out when he's able. We'll need the information as soon as possible to treat her properly."

She gives him a pen as Grace is wheeled down the hallway, away from the ER. From a distance away, Brett is pacing and watching them, his prosthetic hand down the pocket of his coat—out of sight.

The nurse continues, bending slightly to pat John on his shoulder. "Don't worry, sir, we'll do everything we can." John nods. "There have been a lot of overdoses in the past few weeks, so we're well equipped to handle it."

"…thank you," John replies.

The nurse walks away, and Paul gently pulls John up off the floor and towards the waiting room. He hands over the paperwork when they sit, and takes them back to the desk when John's done filling.

Brett's standing in one corner of the waiting room when Paul sits beside John again.

"I don't understand," John says. "Why didn't it work? All the people you've helped, and it didn't work when I needed it the most?"

"I think I know why," Paul responds carefully. John looks at him. "I don't think you're going to like the answer."

"Just tell me, Paul."

Paul wrings his hands. "…I don't think the overdose was an accident…"

John's confused at first, but understanding slowly shows on his face; it makes his face slack. "My daughter did not try to kill herself, Paul. That's…you're wrong."

"Maybe." Paul shrugs. "But everybody else we've helped has been hurt by somebody else. The woman who had a heart attack didn't want to, but she had no control over it. The only difference between all of them and Grace could very well be—"

"Enough!" John gets up. It must have been hard on her. Grace might have been troubled, needed him, and he hadn't been able to see that. But…but, it was just…too much. No, he's not going to assume anything, so he draws a shaky breath and walks away.

They go to her hospital room when she wakes up. A bit drowsy, she's still snarky enough to roll her eyes when John walks through the door and pulls her hand away when he immediately goes to hold it.

"I'm glad you're okay, Grace," John says even though she's looking at him with cold, bitter eyes.

When Lily comes, she showers Grace with light hugs and kisses, feeling her face, legs, and hands, making sure they're fine.

"I'm okay, Mom," Grace says.

"What happened?" When Lily asks, Grace looks away.

The Floor nurse enters. "Okay, Mom and Dad," she says, "let's give her some room. She needs meds and rest." Grace doesn't look back when the nurse ushers them all out of the room.

# SEVEN

Lily and John are sitting on the chairs lined along the walls of the hallway outside Grace's bedroom. They're both tired and relieved. Paul glares at them both from his seat across from them.

They don't look at each other, but Paul watches Lily cross her ankles towards John, and John leans on the armrest towards Lily. Their silence makes him look between the both of them before pulling himself up.

"I'm gonna stop at the restroom real quick," he says, "You guys need anything? Coffee? Water?"

"No, thank you." Lily's voice is thin.

John's voice is just as worn. "Thank you, Paul. I'm fine."

When Paul walks up the hallway and takes the first corner he comes across, Lilly glances at John and takes a deep breath. She puts her hand on his. He looks at it, at her, surprised, hopeful.

"Thank you, John...for calling me."

"Of course. What else could I have done?"

"Well, you could have…not. You could have told me after the fact, so you could be the only one here when she woke up."

The very idea disgusts John, and he scrunches his face.

"Or, you could have never told me about this," she continues, "pretended she was at a friend's house or hanging out with you, and this would be a terrible secret that you and she shared. You could have done a lot of things."

John blinks at her, placing his other hand over hers. "Lily, where is this coming from? Do you really think I would act like that?"

"Working for a family court, I hear these kinds of stories all day. How nasty people are to one another. It's like they've never met, let alone loved one another. Like they hate each other".

He squeezes her hand. "I could never hate you, Lily."

"I don't hate you either…not all the time."

John laughs. Lily reaches into her bag and pulls out the envelope with the divorce paperwork. "I was literally about to drop this in the mailbox when my phone rang. Seems like a sign."

"I would say an act of God."

"I keep thinking that maybe I'm making an emotional decision. You always said never to do that. I just can't seem to be settled with the decision."

"I thought this was what you wanted."

"I don't know what I want, John."

John pauses for a moment, glancing at the armrest where his hand had held hers. "…can we…hold off on it a bit?"

Lily considers it before giving him a small smile. "At least, you can still read my mind."

Lily hugs him, it's warm, and John smiles at it before seeing Paul's head peeking around the corner—he has a thumb up. John's smile broadens, and he gives Paul a thumbs up in return.

Paul is seated in the hallway when John and Lily walk out of Grace's room; he is finishing off a soda and a bag of potato chips. They sit beside him and let out a deep sigh before John's phone chimes and he looks at the screen for a moment.

"Oh, I totally forgot I had a ?bible study tonight."

Lily looks at him, and for a moment, she's about to say something, but she purses her lips and changes her mind. "You should go."

John pauses and looks at her, then at his phone, and at Paul. "Maybe," he says to Lily, "Cher can sit in for me…"

Lily's skeptical. "Are you sure?"

"I can't leave. Not now. Not after coming so close to…I can't."

"I'm impressed, John, but I know how much that means to you, so you should just go."

Paul, done with his snack, gets up and stretches. "Why don't I go? I could help Cher."

It catches John off-guard, but his lips twitch into a smile. "Why, thank you, Paul. Are you sure?"

"Yeah, how hard can it be? I've been studying and making notes."

With a smile, John nods and takes out his car keys from his pocket. "Alright. Do you have a license and everything? I don't want you getting arrested running an errand."

The keys make Paul begin hyperventilating slightly. He shakes his head at them. "It's fine. I can walk."

"It's at least seven miles, Paul."

"I walk really fast. Maybe I'll even just grab a cab."

Paul quickly takes his bag and leaves. John and lily exchange confused looks.

"What was that about?" Lily asks.

"I'm not sure…" John answers, his eyes narrowing as he watches Paul disappear down the hallway.

At the backseat of the taxi, Paul stares out the window, clutching his bag tightly to his chest.

*He's driving, his eyes dilated from drinking. His fiancée, Priya, is seated in the driver's seat, with horror in her eyes. She reaches for Peter strapped in the baby seat on the back seat of the car. A truck's headlights illuminate the interior of the car, its horn blazing…*

The phantom noise of the memory startles him—Priya's horrific scream.

The taxi driver's glancing at him through the rear-view mirror. "You okay there, buddy?"

"Yeah." Paul swallows and nods. "I'm fine."

# EIGHT

Paul enters the fellowship hall. It's a small room, and Cher's already setting up a circle of folding chairs at the front of the room. There's a folding table draped in white linen cloth and stacked with snacks and drinks.

Cher raises her head when she hears the door. "Grab Bibles on your way here, please, Paul."

He obeys without a word, carrying as many Bibles as he can before hefting them down the aisle to her.

"One on each chair," she instructs. "Great. Looks like we're all set then. Why couldn't the pastor be here? He didn't say." She's standing upright and asking him, her head tilted as she watches Paul's expression.

"Are you okay?" she asks.

"Grace is in the hospital. She overdosed."

Cher is stricken, and Paul grabs her to help her to a chair and is thrown into a vision.

*He and Cher are dressed in wedding clothes, racing barefooted and happy through an open field towards a beautiful waterfall.*

*They are in bed together; Paul is reading from a Bible, with Cher leaning against his chest listening.*

*She's feeding a child as Paul hurriedly kisses them and rushes off to work.*

When he snaps out of it, Cher's seated. "What happened?" She's staring at him with watchful eyes, and Paul's confused for a moment, unsure how to respond. "What happened to Grace?"

Carefully, Paul answers, "She...overdosed...on pills."

The response hits Cher, and she closes her eyes and allows her head to sag.

"But it's okay." Paul tries to reassure her. "The doctor said she's going to be alright with a little bit of time."

The reassurance doesn't go very well because Cher looks like she's going to throw up.

"Are you okay?" Paul asks. "You seem to be taking this real hard."

Cher sighs. "You could say that."

"I'm sorry. I feel like we got off on the wrong foot when we first met, and now I've upset you with bad news. I apologize. I can go wait in the office until you're finished with the group—"

"That won't be necessary. I know you're here to help. I'm sorry I gave you the impression you'd done something wrong. I'm the one with issues."

Paul hands her a bottle of water from the snack table. "Issues?"

"I've been where you are. That's how I started working here in the first place." She takes a sip and wipes her mouth with the back of her hand. "Living on the streets, nowhere to go, no aim in life, taking every drug I could get my hands on, doing whatever with whoever for money; the whole gamut."

Cher hangs her head again. "I saw my past in Grace from the day I met her. I saw the hurt, the darkness. I would never wish that for her, but I"d be lying if I said I couldn't have seen it coming. I thought it would be better for her since she had a pastor for a father and a mother working in a court and understanding what dysfunction looks like." She shakes her head and raises it, making eye contact with Paul.

"But," he offers, "it didn't go any better."

"Apparently. So when you told me, it just brought back a lot of memories that I thought I'd forgotten. That could have been me, except I wouldn't have anyone to care for me."

"I care."

"This is the product. You should have known me when I was going through the process."

"I could say the same thing."

"The first time I saw you, fresh off the street, it took me back to that place. That must have been how I'd looked to pastor John when he'd reached out to me. When I needed a job so that I could stay off the streets, he gave me that. I was just uncomfortable to see you, to be reminded of that. I'm sorry."

It makes Paul smile. "Please, don't apologize. We all have issues." He sees Cher waiting for him to continue, waiting for him to tell his story. He draws a deep breath. "My...my mom was an addict. She sold herself to fund her addiction. I was...well, I am a child of a lifetime of bad decisions, a product of rape. She despised me, said I reminded her of my father..."

His eyes seem distant; he can see her, *his mother, Marie, lying unconscious on the bathroom floor with a needle in her hand and foam coming out of her mouth. Her eyes turned over in her head.*

"I was only seven when I found her on our bathroom floor, dead. She'd overdosed."

He remembers standing at the doorway, staring down at his mother's dead body. Cher's eyes mimic the pain of his childhood. "A child should never have to go through that," she says with a small voice.

"I felt responsible. Going in and out of foster care, my own life became a series of bad choices. Though I made some good ones, they just couldn't compensate for the wrong decisions I made."

"You were a child, Paul. You shouldn't blame yourself for that."

"John wanted me to drive his car here, but I couldn't. Every time I see a child, I have to turn away. At least you've forgotten, I can't forget." Cher's brow knot closer together. She's perplexed.

"What do you mean?"

Paul walks to the opposite side of the room, away from her, and holds on to the back of a folding chair. His fingers are working to flick something on the back of the chair, and he looks down at it, not needing to look Cher in the eyes.

"I was driving drunk with my fiancée and two-year-old son in the car," he starts. "I crashed and killed them—five years ago. I haven't driven since."

Cher gets up and comes to him, comes close. Paul tries to get away from her, taking a step back, but her hand on his shoulder stops him.

The contact makes him float in and out of a vision.

*Translucent Cher in heaven glancing in his direction.*

"I'm so sorry, Paul," she says. "I can't imagine how painful that must have been for you. I appreciate you trusting me with that."

Paul looks at her, looks into her eyes.

*Translucent Cher running around and playing with spirit children.*

"I'm a murderer," he whispers as a response.

"It was an accident."

*She's jumping through dimensions, an explosion of color and beauty.*

"I had been drinking. I knew my fiancée could have driven easily, she should have been the one driving, but I'd guilted her into letting me drive. I killed them both. That's on my hands."

Cher pulls him into an embrace. The vision fades away, leaving Paul with a moment. Tears swell in his eyes, and he hugs her back. The door opens and members start coming in. He and Cher pull away from each other and compose themselves.

The Bible study goes great. Often, throughout Bible study, Paul and Cher lock eyes from across the room and exchange childish smiles. It's a pleasant feeling, and somehow, they're both filled with happiness that they chuckle on the seats for no reason at all and have to mutter apologies when the members of the Bible study glance at them.

After the Bible study, they start to work together. Cher has always had to help out with preparing for events, and since Paul joined, he's been helping out whenever he had the chance, but now it's a bit different. There's a more natural teamwork pattern where they work together almost in sync. They help out with Sunday service in the church and sit next to each other on the bus during a church trip. There's no awkward silence, or discomfort, just easy companionship that could have made anybody wonder how long they'd known each other. Cher helps Paul sort through paperwork, playfully teasing him as she aids him through. When Grace gets discharged from the hospital, they both help John and Lily decorate for Grace's "Welcome Home" party, and it is obvious to both John and Lily how much the relationship between Paul and Cher has blossomed.

# NINE

Cher and Paul are sitting at the dining table, a board of chess between them. Cher jumps three pieces in a row and grins. It's flustering, and Paul is trying to figure out how that jump happened while she laughs at him.

Cher sips from her glass of wine. "Don't worry, I'll tell everyone you're letting me win."

Paul sighs and leans back into his chair. "I can take my loss with dignity," he says with a shrug.

"—losses..."

Paul laughs, "Whatever."

"It's all about being a few steps ahead, that's all. Thinking further into the future than what's on the board in front of you."

The smile on his face falls. "...It's definitely been a while since I did that..."

"Then do it."

"What?"

"Do it right now." Cher gets up and starts to pack up the game. "What's in store for you? What do you want? Where are you headed, Paul Samson?"

Paul sighs again. "I…really don't know. I feel like I'm just treading water until we get married, then I'll have to take it from there."

Cher gives him a look like he's suddenly a strange, unfamiliar thing sitting in her apartment. "Excuse me?"

"I know it's kind of weird for me to be a grown man and have no idea, but…I don't know. That's where I am right now. It took me so long to even get to a place where—"

"—you said *when we get married*." Her voice is calm, but her expression isn't. Paul winces at his obvious mistake, but he can't think of how to correct it. Nothing to say. "So, you've apparently thought far ahead enough that you think of me accepting your proposal as a predetermined conclusion."

The words to explain aren't coming. Cher snatches the wine glass and the closed game off the table. "You didn't need to consult with me about it in any manner whatsoever. I should have known better; I deserve this for getting involved with somebody I knew was just like me—the old me." She pours herself some more wine after putting the checkers' box on the bookshelf.

Paul gets up. "Cher, I'm not—"

She's gesturing wildly with her occupied hands, wine slushing as she waves the glass around. "—I mean, you just know for a fact that it's going to happen. Wait…" Cher pauses and gives him a look. "Oh no, was that your proposal? Did you just ask me to marry you saying it was a sure thing?" She stalks towards him as she talks, and he backs away into the dining table with his hands up, knocking his glass of water over.

"I…I had a vision, that's all. I didn't make assumptions about what you want."

Cher stops inches away from him and chews her bottom lip for a few seconds.

Paul's eyes fall to the ground. "I… uh… I should go…" he manages.

"Yeah…" Cher's voice is a whisper. "Good night, Mr. Samson." She walks away, into her kitchenette.

Paul picks up the glass and starts to reach for paper towels.

"Just leave it and go," Cher says, watching him from the kitchenette.

He goes to stand next to her. "Cher, I didn't mean—"

"Just," she barks out, her voice thick and her eyes wet, "go." She turns her back to him and covers her face.

Paul stands forlorn for several moments before grabbing his coat and keys and leaving her to herself.

She doesn't call him over the weekend, and when he calls, her phone just rings, she never picks up.

When Monday rolls around and they are both at the fellowship prepping the sleeping area with volunteers, Paul keeps looking across the cavernous room at her, hoping that she'll at least look his way and see how sorry he is in his eyes. They clean the bunks, clean the railings, sweep, and wipe the door handles, but Cher never once looks up. Never glances his way. She's helping out with things that don't point in his direction, and it hurts a little and makes Paul sigh loudly, as if John hadn't already caught on enough.

"What happened to you two?" John asks, "It's like a morgue in here."

He hadn't noticed, but when Paul glances around, he sees it; the tension in the volunteers' bodies as they work. They look away when they glance and find him watching. They're casting looks between him and Cher, talking softly even while they're turned away from him.

Paul clears his throat. "I, uh, accidentally let her know that I knew we were going to get married."

John's eyebrows shoot up.

"Yeah, I had a vision, and I…I just somehow lost consciousness that it hadn't happened yet."

The surprise doesn't last, and John frowns at him. "Let me guess; she felt like she didn't have a choice. Like you thought it was set in stone. Well, besides the fact that you sound like you're hallucinating."

Paul sighs. "Pretty much. She kicked me out of her apartment a couple of days ago and hasn't spoken to me since. She doesn't take my calls, never talks to me when she sees me; it's like we're strangers now."

John nods. "I can relate *very well* to being shut out."

Paul continues making the beds again. "I'm sorry, I know this is nothing compared to a divorce."

"It's not about comparing, Paul. Pain is pain. Heartbreak is heartbreak. I'm just saying that I've been there and I understand. She'll come around, don't worry." John puts a comforting hand on Paul's shoulder.

*Paul, John, Lily, and a few others are all dressed in black and standing over a casket at a cemetery. A pastor is reading from a book. Paul is glaring at an enlarged picture of Grace positioned among flowers, above the casket.*

John's still talking. "...this is just one of the benefits of faith. Less stress!" He grins at Paul and notices how shaken up he is. He notices his hands. "What did you see?"

Paul doesn't reply. He's still lost in the trance.

"Paul, tell me what you saw."

Paul blinks and looks at John. "I...uh...it's probably nothing."

John's about to say something, but his phone rings; it's Grace. He answers it and uses his other hand to smoothen out the sheet he just put on the bed in front of him. "Hello, dear."

Grace's voice is low, and it sounds like she has been crying. "Please, dad, come get me."

John hears people arguing in the background. He straightens, taps Paul on the shoulder, and heads towards the exit, motioning for him to follow. "Grace, who's that yelling in the background?"

Paul frowns as they go.

"Where are you?"

The car is parked on the street outside the fellowship. "Near the pizza shop on 7<sup>th</sup> street, in the alley. Hurry, dad." Her voice hushes down to a whisper. John is hyperventilating as if he can feel the darkness around him thicken and suck the air from his lungs. He has not heard Grace call him "dad" in years. He fights to keep the negative thoughts at bay.

"Grace, what's going on? Why are you whispering?"

Gunshots fire in the background, two shots, and the phone abruptly disconnects. John stares at his phones for a moment when the call's cut, his eyes are wide and afraid when they rise to meet Paul's. They're asking a question in them that Paul isn't sure he should answer. Then, like a snap, he comes to his senses and rushes for his car, leaving Paul to follow after him. John starts the car even before Paul has settled in and screeches off up the street while Paul struggles to close the door as they move.

John's swerving from lane to lane, avoiding cars but not allowing anyone to slow him down.

Paul asks, "What did she say? Who was yelling at her?"

John's grip on the steering tightens, his knuckles whitening. "I don't know, but I heard shots."

Paul and John pull up in the nearest parking space along the street in front of the pizza parlor. The police sirens are loud and quickly approaching, it makes them give each other a scared look before running up to the mouth of the alley.

Mac rounds a corner at the end of the block, Paul barely catching a glimpse of him before he's gone. When they turn into the alley, Grace is on the ground, in a pool of blood.

The police cars have pulled up behind them. Brett and a few other officers jump out, one of them speaking into a radio.

"We need an EMT at Priory Pizza immediately. We've got one young woman down. Possible gunshot wound."

Paul is already on his knees beside Grace, recovered from the shock and extending a hand to her, but an officer pulls him from the ground before he can touch her.

John's shouting. "Officer, he can help. Allow him to do something!"

Brett steps forward and bends to check for her pulse. He frowns, sighs, and shakes his head at the other officers. "She's gone."

Paul quickly looks up to Grace's translucent body ascending above them. She's smiling at him as her form dissipates into thin air.

John's still talking, "Officer, please, just let Paul help her."

"She's gone, John."

He's still yelling. "Gone where? She's right there, Paul. All you have to do is touch her."

Brett stands up. "Nobody is touching anybody today. You're both coming with us."

One of the officers starts to read Paul his Miranda rights, but John lunges at him and is immediately blocked and restrained by another officer.

"Leave him alone," John's still trying, "he can save her. That's my daughter!"

Paul is placed in the back of a cruiser and driven away. John watches in panic.

"Calm down, sir," an officer says, "EMTs are on the way."

John is handcuffed. Brett gives him a disdainful look. "Your own daughter, pastor? How sick are you?"

John breaks free from the officer restraining him, his hands still cuffed, and goes to Grace's body.

"Grace, I know you can hear me. It's going to be okay. Just hang in there."

"Get him to the station. I'll wait here for the ambulance."

John looks up at Brett. "I need to call my wife."

Another officer gets control over John again to force him into the back of the squad car, but he struggles the entire time, screaming and fighting.

"That's my daughter!"

He twists and turns around in the back seat, crying out for Grace as they speed away from the alley, from her dead body.

Chapter
# TEN

The car drives past an alley, and Paul sees Mac again, tossing something behind a dumpster in the alley. He slams his head against the barrier between him and the front seat of the car.

The officer driving looks up at the rear-view mirror at Paul, observing him with a frown, opening his mouth to say something because Paul seems familiar, a face from a random video he'd been shown by his teenage daughter, but he thought better of it and decided to say something else. "Keep it down back there." His eyes were still on Paul for a while longer as the other man settles into the backseat uncomfortably, eyes misting into a daydream far away from the car. The officer looks away, wondering if it'd have been better to have just asked.

At the station, Brett is sitting across from Paul in the interrogation room, with a two-way mirror beside them and a camera in each corner. The door is behind Brett and one of Paul's cuffed hands is attached to a hook in the center of the table.

Brett only has his organic hand on the tabletop. He opens a file and begins to take out pictures of Paul and John at every crime scene.

"What kind of scheme are you two running?" he asks.

Paul sighs. "I told you, there is no scheme."

"People lie to me all the time, Mr. Samson. Just because you say something doesn't make it true, does it?"

"I don't know what you want me to say, officer. My answer is not going to change because it's the truth." Paul looks at the ground and frowns. "You should have let me help her. That was his only child."

"So, we're back to the things that you say not necessarily being true."

"You knew that was his daughter. You were there in the emergency room with us."

"I don't know anything except what you tell me. You both put on quite a show, but she could have been an accomplice. A mule. A dealer. A whore—"

Paul shoots up, pulling against his restraints, sneering at Brett. "You watch your mouth, *sir*."

A brow goes up. "Or what?"

Paul pauses, breathes deep, and sits back down.

Brett continues. "Seems like she meant a lot to you, huh? Some kind of trafficking ring then? She was a pretty woman."

Paul looks away and shakes his head.

Brett slams his hand on the table.

*Brett is dead. His hair is greying, wrinkles on his face, he looks older, maybe in his 40s or 50s. He's slumped over the kitchen table in his apartment where he must have been in the middle of cleaning his gun.*

*The apartment is barely furnished. The walls are bare, except for various commendations related to his work on the force and the picture of his younger self hugging a young woman holding up a fishing rod with a small silverfish on the hook. No other pictures are there.*

"Who is the young woman?" Paul asks.

"Excuse me?"

"The woman you're hugging in the photo on the wall of your apartment. She caught a small silver fish. It's the only photo you have in the house."

Brett's face is that of surprised…the kind that makes you speechless for a while. "Have you been to my apartment?"

"Yes, just now, but not exactly just now, more like a time in the future."

"What kind of freakshow is this?"

Paul wipes his brow on his shoulder. He's exhausted, emotionally and physically. "You want the truth? You think you can handle the truth? That's how I know what's going to happen. I can see the world without time. You were always a step or two behind because you had to wait on someone to notify the dispatcher and then wait for the dispatcher to tell you."

Brett's face twists into a frown. "See, I've asked you nicely to drop the insanity act, but I see you're going to stick to it. If that's the case, I'll just go ahead and cycle through my normal interrogation points if you don't mind."

"By all means."

Brett shakes his head at Paul, exasperated and annoyed. "Who was telling you that these incidents were going to take place?"

"God."

"God?"

"Yessir. What else did you want me to say?"

"What's in it for you? Why are you hurting people? And how were you able to convince the leader of one of the most helpful churches in the neighborhood to work with you? Transport you? How'd you do that?"

"I can see."

"So can I, and I can recognize a fraud when I see one. Your tricks won't work on me."

"I saw you in your apartment, dead. Very little furniture, one photograph, and some recognition from the force. You died at the dinner table while cleaning your gun, and nobody was there with you."

"Most people on the force die a violent death, so I guess I'm not rocking the boat."

"You've seen for yourself what God has done through me. Why don't you believe?" His eyes shift to the side of the table, where Brett is hiding his prosthetic hand. "What happened to your hand?"

Brett's eyes narrow. "What's that to you?"

"Do you want your hand back?"

Brett burst out laughing. "Now, that's something I haven't seen in all my years on the force; a criminal willing to use my injury to try and persuade me that he's not full of crap."

"I can give you your hand back, sir."

Brett rolls his eyes but doesn't move his hand. "Whatever you say, Mr. Miracle Worker. Just give it up and tell me the truth."

Paul sighs. "At least let John go. Let him be with his wife and say goodbye to his little girl. You know you have no reason to hold us."

Brett gets up. "I don't know what it is with you. Psychosis? Under the influence? Developmental disability?" He shrugs. "It's about time for my shift to end anyway. Why don't you grab one of our honeymoon suites and I'll see you in the morning, hmm?"

Bret opens the door and calls for an officer. A picture of Mac is among the photos scattered on the table. Paul reaches for it and touches it.

Brett's voice even breaks through the vision. "Put him in a holding cell. I'll be back for a second date tomorrow."

*It's not the station, it's the alley, and Mac is there arguing with a man with Grace trying to pull the man away. He snatches his arm from her and pulls a gun out from the back of his pants to point it at Mac.*

*Mac freezes, looking angry, and Grace tries to get the gun away from the man. The gun goes off and Grace falls to the ground, blood flowing from a wound. Mac is frozen with shock; the man drops the gun, horrified, and runs off.*

*A store owner comes around the corner, sees what's happened, calls the police, and runs back into the pizza place. Mac is still stunned for a while more before he quickly picks up the gun and takes off, walking briskly to not draw attention to himself.*

Brett is still saying something. "—I don't have enough to hold you for long just yet, but believe me, I'll be looking. The second I find something on you or your pastor friend, you'll both be real cozy in the county, real fast."

An officer uncuffs Paul from the table after Brett leaves. Paul is dazed as the officer leads him away. "What have I done?"

At processing, Paul is getting his belongings from a woman at the window. There is a line of people waiting to get their possessions and leave and an officer standing guard to keep things in order. It's crowded but calm.

The woman gives Paul his things in a plastic bag, and he empties them into his pockets. "Excuse me, ma'am, I was wondering if you could tell me what happened to Pastor John Williams. Was he released?"

The woman looks from him to the trail of people behind him waiting to be released. She shrugs and types on her computer. "Looks like he was released yesterday."

"Thank you."

## ELEVEN

At the cemetery, everything stands still as the pastor reads the final rights. John, Cher, and Lily are there, their heads bowed, their shoulders shuddering. Paul isn't. He's in the distance, under the shade of an overgrown tree. John looks around for him, finds him, and looks away.

After the burial, John leads a grieving Lily to the car, ensures she's seated before walking over to Paul. Neither of them makes eye contact.

"You saw this, didn't you?"

Paul nods solemnly.

"You could have saved her, Paul. She was our only daughter." John walks away, back to his car, and drives off. In the distance, Cher glances in Paul's direction before turning away and leaving as well. Everybody leaves, but Paul's still there; standing under the tree with his face in his hands and his shoulders shuddering as he cries.

Paul sits on the ground in the alley where he used to sleep. There's a backpack beside him. He raises his head and looks at the sky and sees heaven open to reveal a garden.

*Paul's soul walks towards a bridge where the Son of God is standing, waiting for him...*

It's the alley, it's a different day, but he's still there. There's a bottle in the brown paper bag he's holding, and he downs its content. He empties the bottle and reaches for more in his backpack, opens and empties that one too.

When he raises his head and looks at the sky, he sees what everybody else sees; a dark sky with a partial moon and countless stars. He gives it a drunken smile. "That's much better. No John, no Cher, no job, no visions. Life is perfect. No pain, no worries. It's all melting away. Completely away...just the way I like it."

It's a bar, it's afternoon so the place isn't packed. Paul is barely balanced on a bar stool, there're four empty beer bottles in front of him, and he's working on the fifth. The bartender is giving him a look as he continues to slur his words.

"—and another thing that people don't understand is that the gift—if you help people—its consequences aren't always good, you know..." He turns to the man on the stool beside him. "If I hadn't given Mac his legs, he wouldn't have been able to do drugs. Grace wouldn't have gotten mixed up in all that mess, and she wouldn't have gotten shot."

The man gets up and walks away, so Paul turns to the person on his other side.

"See, he doesn't get it. The truth is, if we hadn't saved Grace's life the first time, she never would have been there. John could have lost her once instead of twice." He makes gestures with his fingers, he's trying for a two, but not quite getting it. "Do you know what it feels like to lose one person two times?"

Paul starts to cry, and the people around him are immediately visibly uncomfortable.

"...and Priya too. I killed them..."

The bartender draws a breath and tries. "Hey buddy, maybe it's time you took a little break, yeah?"

Paul nods unsteadily and slowly slides off the barstool. He picks up his backpack and looks at the Bartender, tears still streaming from his eyes. "But...but...what is the point of helping people if no good can come from it?"

The bartender gives him a soft look. "I don't know, man, maybe there's no point. Maybe you'll figure it out when you dry out, yeah? Go on now."

Still crying, Paul shuffles out of the bar, people giving him a wide berth as he passes. He starts to sing as he leaves.

"Swing low, sweet cherio..."

Days pass with him sleeping and waking up under cardboard pieces. Sometimes another homeless person sits in the alley with him, the both of them surrounded by empty beer bottles. When he manages to find enough money, he squanders it in bars until he's asked to leave—he's usually asked to leave. Sometimes he doesn't go, it's too hard to get up and find his way back to the alley, but then they get physical and throw him out of the bar—they usually throw him out of the bar. If it rains, he sits in it and allows it to drench him. He has no umbrella, no coat. If kids come around to throw trash at him, he sits and lets them. He has no care, not about anything, not anymore.

# TWELVE

For John, the days are crawling by.

He's looking through the closet for a shirt, when he fails to find one, he goes back to kiss Lily who's lying as if she's asleep—she isn't—then he grabs a stray shirt and pulls it on in front of the vanity. He looks so dreary he tries to smile, but somehow it looks even worse. It looks forced, weak.

His feet carry him to Grace's room, her former room. Everything is still in place as if she's out with a friend or at school, as if she'll come back any minute now and roll her eyes at the sight of him standing in her room. He would much prefer that than her not being there.

When he goes to stand in the center of the room, it starts to spin. The scents are too strong, the place is too warm. On her desk is her laptop, still opened, her bedsheet are rumpled, they're black and white, on her nightstand is a lamp, it's shaped like a bat.

"…oh, Grace…" John says with a sigh, his eyes closed.

It's too much, and he rushes out with his chin quivering. The tears have swollen up in his eyes, and he's shaking his head to keep them away.

In the living room, the area around the couch is spotless, and the coffee table is clear of anything except the television remote, a worn Bible, and an invoice for the retainer fee of a divorce lawyer.

John sighed at it. She hasn't filed the paperwork, but she hasn't gotten rid of the lawyer either. It's too much, so he goes outside and breathes in deeply. He needs to be somewhere else.

It is a bit easier to breathe at the fellowship. Cher knocks on the frame of the opened door.

"Hey."

John sees her and smiles. "Hello Cher, Sorry for the extended—"

"Don't do that. Please. You took as much time as you needed to. It's a tragedy."

Her eyes are intense, so John looks away and nods. He clears his throat after a while. "What can I do for you?"

"I was coming to ask you the same thing. Coffee? Tea? Have you even eaten?"

"I'm...I'm fine. Is there anything else? Something I need to know? Is everything running smoothly?"

"Well...that's virtually never the case..." They both chuckle. "...but, I've handled most of the small fires, so we're okay, I think."

"Thank you, Cher, it means a lot to have someone be able to help while I—as we're going through this as best as we can…"

"Of course. Well, let me know if you think of anything, and I'll get right on it."

"Actually," John starts, looking at Cher uncertainly, "I just came from the shelter, looking for Paul…"

Cher's face falls.

"I know the two of you haven't been on good terms, I understand, but I'm just concerned about him. I haven't heard from him."

"Well…maybe he thought you needed your space…"

"I agree, but I've gotten cards, emails, texts, flowers, and even visits regardless. It just seems odd that he would kind of fall off the face of the earth like this. Have you seen him?"

Cher bites her lip and shakes her head. "No, sir."

John frowns. "So, something could be wrong?"

Cher starts to look a bit worried. "I guess so."

John gets up. "I've got to go find him. I just hope it isn't too late." He doesn't miss the look on Cher's face as he leaves.

John searches as he drives, squinting at passers-by as he saddles along sidewalks, accidentally calling out to strangers twice. He searches alleys and bars, talking to the bartenders, and even driving to clinics and speaking with nurses who weren't in enough of a rush to ignore him. Nothing turns up, but he keeps searching, hopefully, Paul hasn't gone too far.

He finds Paul in the evening. He's a distance away from John, in an alley, and it looks as if he's settling down for a nap. By the time John parks his car and gets close, Paul's already curled up and sleeping, empty and broken bottles around him—cheap alcoholic drinks. Paul's drunk, so he doesn't even shake when John struggles to pick him up and drape him over his shoulder.

*Translucent John is crouched by what seems like a sea of crystals. Soul Paul approaches from behind and crouches beside him.*

*"I saw your true celestial form, it was divine." Soul Paul says.*

*"Father has made us glorious beings to radiate His glory through creation."*

*"What a gift!"*

*Translucent John chuckles. "Imagine, we go to earth and forget."*

*"But why do we forget?"*

*"We enter a fallen world to redeem His glory. Divine realities can only be introduced through divine revelation.*

*It must be accessed through knowledge and faith, and manifested through intention."*

*"The will of man?"*

*"The will of man in creation was meant to be the will of God in eternity."*

*A beautiful female form with two smaller girls emerges from the sea of crystals and smile at translucent John before floating away.*

*"Who are they?" Soul Paul asks.*

*"My wife and children. The younger is Grace; my firstborn is Joy."*

*"It's hard to fathom sometimes that all that is not yet in time, already is in eternity."*

# Chapter
## THIRTEEN

Paul wakes up in John's living room. His eyes open slowly, and he's lying on a couch with John sitting opposite him waiting. Paul sits up and holds his head.

"Long night?" John asks, sounding a bit amused.

Paul groans. "I have a raging headache."

Lily comes out with two cups of coffee. "Maybe this will help."

She gives them each a cup and sits with John, holding his hand.

Paul stares at the cup in his hands, it's warm. "Why did you...bring me here...?"

"I couldn't leave you on the streets."

"Why not? It's where I belong." Paul takes a sip from his cup and puts it down. "I need to go."

"You're not going anywhere, Paul," Lily interjects, "You're welcome here."

John gives him a hopeful smile. "The woman of the house has spoken."

Paul looks away, hurt. "It was my fault," he says. "It was my fault that Grace got—hurt."

"It was nobody's fault. She made her choices herself."

Paul pauses and takes a breath.

"What happened to your firstborn?" he asks.

Lily looks away with an odd expression, her grip on John's hand loosens.

"What are you talking about?" John asks, "We have only one child."

"Grace is your second child. I saw them both. Your firstborn was named Joy."

Lily gets up and leaves, and John looks after her confused, glances and Paul, and then gets up after her.

She's standing on the backyard porch looking over the garden, her arms folded and tears streaming down her cheek. She's been crying a lot these days. John comes up behind her.

"Lily, what's going on?"

She doesn't answer, just stares at the garden as she sobs. John goes to her and cups her shoulders in his hands. "Please," he says softly, "talk to me."

"You were on the verge of going into ministry. We were young, unmarried, John, we weren't ready for a child. I saw how much ministry meant to you, so I made a choice."

John's breathing shakes.

"…I had an abortion."

"You made that decision all by yourself?" His hands fall off her shoulders.

Lily bows her head and sobs. "…I'm so sorry…"

John looks at her, by his face, he's hurt by what she's just admitted. That she had kept something like that from him for all these years, it makes him step back, but he also starts to reach forward on reflex to comfort her before he stops himself and puts his hand down. Maybe what he needs is a few moments to gather himself. He nods and goes away without another word.

It's just sometime past noon, so the bar isn't yet rowdy. Its musky interior ladled with hardwood floors and the distinct waft of strong liquor is a subtle comfort for the few patrons inside. There's very little hubbub, so the bartender has the television on and the volume up to compensate. It's reshowing one of the previous week's games.

Paul and John are there, seated at the counter next to each other, a bottle of beer in front of them each.

"What I'm able to do is a curse, not a gift. At least, I can't do it as long as I'm drinking."

Johns looks at his bottle, tries for a sip, and ends up putting it aside. "It's better to know than not know. We both need to get back on the right path."

"I've caused you nothing but pain."

"No more than what Jesus went through for us."

"So, you're saying you can forgive your wife for what she did?"

"I already did, before I even knew it. If I've learned anything from you, it's that I'm better than who I am now. If I keep doing what's right, I'll become better."

Paul lets out a short laugh. "I wish you could see yourself in the spirit, John; it's a glorious sight to behold."

John gives him a small smile. "I don't have to see to believe anymore, my friend. Meeting you, seeing the things you do, that has impacted me in more ways than you know."

"I still couldn't save her, John, I can't forgive myself for that."

Paul finishes his beer, grabs his backpack, and walks out the door. John drinks his beer, just a small sip, and spits it back out. His face twists in disgust at the taste. "How do people drink this stuff?" Then he goes after Paul.

It's raining outside. Paul's walking without an umbrella or a coat. John pulls alongside him, driving slowly.

"Get in the car, Paul."

"No, thanks. Just leave me alone."

"You know that's not going to happen," John says as somebody behind him honks. He waves that the car should go around him. "I'll be beside you until you either get in or get to where you're going." He follows Paul for a few blocks, cars behind him honking before driving around him with curses and obscenities being thrown at him.

"I'm sure the police will be here soon; somebody must have called them by now. We might get to see our friend, Officer Brent, again."

Paul stops, his shoulders sagging, the idea of seeing the officer again is more unpleasant than the cold. It doesn't even compare despite the rain beating down against his head and shoulders. Weary, he lets out a heavy breath and gets in the car, ignoring John's playful and heavily satisfied smirk.

The fellowship is warm. The room John leads Paul into is clean and furnished with a table, a chair, and a cell phone. A Bible rests on the table beside the phone.

"What's this?" Paul asks, looking around.

"This room was not really being used, so we decided to make a space for you."

"You did this for me?"

"To be honest, Cher did most of it. I had the idea, she executed."

Paul looks at him with bright eyes and a small awkward smile.

"Thank you, John. I…don't know what to say. This is…this is amazing."

John hands Paul the key to the room, and also the cell phone. "The job is still yours as well."

Paul purses his lips for a moment and smiles. "I could use a raise."

"Don't push it."

Paul looks over the phone. "I don't know if I still remember how to use one of these…"

"It was the devil of a time finding you. I'd rather not spend that much time or gas in the future."

Paul smiles and tries to say something, but he keeps coming up blank. John chuckles at him. "It's okay, Paul, I know."

Cher comes in, and Paul isn't sure how to look at her as she makes her way to him with take-out in her hands.

"I thought you might be hungry." She smiles at him as he glares at her with soft, wet eyes. She places the take-out in his hand, and walks away.

John's voice barely breaks through to him as he stares at the door, after Cher. "Eat and rest. We'll talk later."

John puts a hand on Paul's shoulder, and Paul holds on to his wrist and squeezes, unable to speak. He braces himself for the vision, but nothing happens. John shuts the door after him when he leaves, and Paul puts everything down and covers his face with his hands.

The day has been so very…overwhelming.

# FOURTEEN

*I*n the Realm of Light, Soul Paul is surrounded by infinitesimal portals appearing and disappearing. They're colorful and especially breathtaking against the cosmic background. He's walking with Cheviel, who leads him to a portal and starts telling him a story that the portal begins to play out—in sync with the angel's words.

"A man once had two sons. One son asked his father for his inheritance, truly only owed in the case of his father's death. But the father loved the son and only wanted his happiness, so he allowed it. He gave the son every penny of his inheritance, and—as so often happens—the son frittered the funds away as quickly as he'd got them. He ended up having to do menial labor farming pigs to earn money. It's tough work farming pigs, and it doesn't pay as much as you'd think. It got so bad, he even considered eating from the pig's slop trough."

Paul grimaces at the thought, and Cheviel smiles at him but continues. "He thought to himself, one day "If it's come to this, I might as well go back to my father, beg forgiveness, and maybe become his servant. At least they

117

*are fed better, whatever their circumstances." And so, the son did what he wanted and returned home, ready to humble himself for the rest of his life in hopes of his brazen and indulgent ways being forgiven. Yet, as soon as he was within sight of his father' house, his father came out to greet him, nearly toppling him over. So glad was the father that the son had returned. But the son was shocked and asked, "What is this, Father? I have sinned so much, against heaven and against you, I don't deserve to be called your son any longer. I came to you to beg to be your servant."*

*But his father would hear none of it and made the servants bring fine robes for the son to wear. They brought precious rings for his fingers and sandals for his feet. The father ordered that a fattened calf be slaughtered and the son's return be celebrated with a feast. The father did all this because, to him, his son had been lost and was now found. He had, in essence, died and was now living."*

*"Am I that son?" Paul asks, looking at his translucent hands.*

*"All human beings are that prodigal son," Cheviel answers, "They are born into creation, so they go through the matrix of transcendence in order to govern the created realm as they have helped to govern in the uncreated realm. This is the path of every single human being. So, those who exist in the mind of God become real in the created world. They are all prodigal sons who leave home with an inheritance to squander as they please."*

118

*Cheviel faces Paul. "Unfortunately, most never choose to come back home. The present world is made for many, but the world to come is made for a few."*

*"Broad is the road that leads to destruction, but narrow is the path of life, and few are those who find it."*

*Cheviel nods. "That's it, you got it."*

*"How do I make things right?"*

*"First, I need you to see something," she says as she puts a finger to Paul's chest.*

*It's another vision, here, Grace is still alive, collecting drugs from Mac and another man named Luke. There's a report on the news showing that there's a contaminated shipment of drugs that entered the city. the news shows people acting insanely, destroying things, running around naked, starting fires.*

*Grace and Mac lay dead in an alley, foaming at the mouth, holding a needle in their hands. Other people are dead throughout the city, from the elderly to teenagers, poor and rich, in all parts of the city. The city is on fire, burning, and Melinda stands in the midst, tears streaming down her face as she holds up a lighted match.*

*The vision leaves Paul reeling. "I...I don't understand."*

*"If Grace hadn't died, what you saw would have been a reality already since no man would have intervened to change that possible future."*

*"...what I saw was...real?"*

"It is real only in the realm outside of time for now, but in time, it is still in the future, unless there is another intervention."

"Why me?"

"A better question to ask is, 'Why not you, Paul?'"

Cheviel drifts backward and is slowly consumed by the light. In the distance, another female form approaches. As the figure gets closer, she starts to come into focus. It's Grace. She's radiant in the open light, a smile on her face."

"Grace?" Paul breathes as she closes the distance between them.

"Hi, Paul."

"You're here?"

"Where else was I going to be?"

He's astonished and happy. "H—how?"

"Before my departure, I saw more clearly than I had ever seen. I saw that I was experiencing a culmination of all my bad choices, but also that it was my destiny."

"B—but, we weren't created to die…"

"It's a strange paradox, Paul. Death always produces life. That's what the ancient ones have been trying to teach us; that though they were immortal, they choose death. For there to be a harvest, seeds must be planted, and the seeds must die before they can produce life."

"That explains why superheroes are always willing to give up their lives to save others."

*Grace gives him an astonishingly bright smile. "There are no superheroes, Paul, just men and cowards. Which one will you be?"*

*Suddenly, even before he can answer her question, Grace's form is sucked into the light and creates two separate sparks that widen and begin to take shape. As they form and come into focus, Paul's eyes widen to see his former fiancée, Priya, and their son, Peter.*

*He takes unsteady steps towards them. Priya smiles at him and directs his gaze to their son, whose face is gloriously lit and beaming with pride. Paul looks from Priya to Peter, remorseful.*

*"I—I'm sorry—"*

*Priya stops him with a finger to his lips. "Shush! It's okay, you need to forgive yourself, Paul." His lips tremble under her finger. "You merely played a part in the pain you asked for, the trials you needed to become who you are. You are him, Paul. You are the man who can save a city."*

*He's crying now, tears like diamonds sliding down his translucent face. When he looks at Peter, the being smiles at him.*

*"Three peas in a pod, Daddy."*

*Priya cups Paul's cheek in her hands. "Have courage, Paul. You are eternally loved."*

## Chapter
# FIFTEEN

Paul wakes in his new room at the fellowship. It's as if he's had the most pleasant dream. His eyes open slowly, almost reluctantly, and he finds the room filling up with sunlight filtered through sheer white curtains. A blanket covers him, and his new phone charges on the makeshift nightstand. He sits and faces the window looking into the street, savoring the warm sunlight on his skin.

Somebody knocks at the door, it's John and Cher. John comes in with a large paper bag, and Cher follows with a carrier that has two to-go cups of coffee.

"Good morning, Paul," John says, "We have breakfast if you're up for it."

He is up for it. "Thank you. I'm starving."

John begins to pull sandwiches out of the bag and onto the nightstand. Cher lays down the carrier and pulls the cups from it. When she hands one to Paul, their fingers graze each other. She pulls back gently, leaving Paul looking at her remorsefully.

"I'm sorry, Cher, for what I did to you."

"It's water under the bridge, Paul. I'm just happy that you're okay."

"Yeah," John adds, "you had her sick from worry."

"I was not!"

She grabs a sandwich and her coffee from the nightstand and moves to leave. Paul can't keep his smile off her face; she had worried about him.

"I'll take mine at my desk so you boys can talk." She glances once at Paul and then leaves.

Paul and John eat in silence for a while. Several times, he holds his sandwich out instead of taking a bite, looking absent-mindedly at the ground before raising his eyes to find John watching him. John doesn't push, even though it's obvious Paul wants to say something. Paul holds the sandwich off again, swallows, and just lets it out. "I saw Grace."

John chokes on his sandwich, takes a moment to recover. He clears his throat and nods his head as he regains his composure.

"She's okay," Paul completes, to which John visibly sighs.

"You saw her in heaven?"

"Heaven is home, John. I'm starting to believe that you must really not want to go there to find yourself anywhere else."

John's face is different, both relieved and sad. "My little girl made it home?"

"Yeah, that's the good news."

124

John pauses, eyebrows crinkling. "What's the bad news?"

"Your dreams are prophetic warnings. I have to confront Melinda or this city is going up in flames."

John breathes. "That's like Esther going to the king without being summoned."

"It's a life and death situation, I know. Which is why I'm going alone."

John shakes his head and bites from his sandwich. "There must be another way."

"I have to decide now if I'm going to be a man or a coward."

"What's the difference? All men are cowards."

"A real man knows he's created a little lower than Elohim, so there's nothing to fear."

"I must not be a real man then."

"I need to do this, John."

"Fine," John puts down his half-eaten sandwich. "then I'm coming with you."

Now, Paul's the one shaking his head. "I can't let you risk your life like that. You have more to lose than I do."

"Well then, let's hope it doesn't come to that. We are doing this together, Paul."

Across the street from the industrial park, John parks his car, and they both sit there in silence for a while. It's night and there are only a few people around. Occasionally, small trucks drive pass into the park.

"Well," Paul asks, "what do you think?"

"I still think this is a bad idea."

Paul sighs and flickers his thumb with the other. "I should go in alone."

"That's an even worse idea."

"Think about Lily, John. She's already dealing with the loss of Grace." It's like he's been chastised, John purses his lips and looks out the windscreen.

Paul starts to chew on a fingernail, thinking audibly. "I wonder if there's another entrance or exit…"

"There isn't," John says without looking back at Paul, "unless it's underground. Now that you've mentioned it, even the way this place was built might be because of what she deals in, you know. The park is built in a tear-drop shape, so you have to leave the way you come."

Paul's nodding and breathing slightly louder. "I see. So she only has one exit to worry about, to defend if the need arises."

"That's what I think." Now he turns to look at Paul. "So, your plan is just to walk in there and talk to her, if by some miracle, which I believe might actually happen, you even get to her?"

Paul glances at him nervously. "Do you have a better idea?"

"What will you even say to her?"

"I...I don't know. Maybe just tell her the truth, that the shipment of drugs she has coming in is contaminated. Maybe appeal to her humanity as a businesswoman who doesn't want to lose customers or profits if she can help it."

"I see. Give her some other bone to chew on instead of coming after you. She'll be focused on her supplier, why they've tainted her delivery, and what exactly they've tainted it with."

"Exactly."

They sit in silence for a while and watch as a black SUV with tinted windows pulls into the park.

"You know this will never work."

"Yep, but it's all I've got." Paul takes a deep breath before leaving after the SUV, sneaking under the cover of shadows. John watches in the car, makes the sign of the cross when Paul enters the park and leaves his sight.

"Help us, Lord."

# SIXTEEN

Among a stack of containers, watching the SUV park close to the entrance of the main building, Paul hides behind. The vehicle engine is turned off, and Melinda alights from the car, followed closely by her bodyguard who scans the area quickly.

A large sliding door opens to let them in, and inside, Paul can see more armed men. He draws a breath, whispers encouragement to himself, and starts to make for the building, but a hand slaps over his mouth and pulls him back into the container shadows.

Brett whispers harshly in his ear. "It's me, calm down. Don't make a sound."

Brett has his hand firmly over Paul's mouth, until the latter nods.

Paul turns around and whispers too. "What are you doing here?"

"Me? Me?! I could ask you the same thing. I've got dozens of units ready to move in at my say so. The entire two-mile radius is blanketed. You're the one here ruining our plan. We're here for Melinda."

"Well, me too."

Brett glares at him in the semi-darkness. "So, you *are* working for her? I should have known."

"No. I'm here to convince her not to put out that last shipment of drugs because it's contaminated."

Brett glares in silence for a moment. "Well, you don't have to worry about that. We're here to shut down her entire operation."

"Yes, but are you confident enough that there is not enough corruption in your department to stop these drugs from still getting out on the streets?"

Brett is quiet for a while. "I'm not convinced that you don't work with or for her."

"Do you?"

Brett scoffs. "I will arrest you again, smartass."

"Just give me a chance to talk to her or we are all in trouble. I need you to at least believe that."

"I don't."

Paul looks down at Brett's prosthetic hand. "Maybe this will help." He grabs the arm of the prosthetic hand, and Brett quickly reaches for his gun with the other hand, but he's frozen before he can draw it. His eyes go wide, and he starts to sweat profusely. He looks down at the prosthetic hand and rips it off his wrist.

Bone, veins, muscle, and flesh fill out the form of the whole hand, all the way to the fingernails. Brett's eyes water from the pain and he's shaking, trying not to scream.

Slowly, Brett lifts his arm, flexing his new hand. Now, his tears are flowing freely, and he's speechless.

"Do you believe me now?" Paul asks, looking at Brett expectantly.

Brett doesn't nod. He doesn't even breathe. With his breathing held back, he slowly takes his new hand with his old one; feels the fingernails, the palm, the thumb. Feels how terribly familiar they all are to touch even though there's this strange foreignness to them as well.

"Y—your power is real?" His voice creaks.

Paul shakes his head. "No, God is real. His thoughts towards you are perfect, complete, not partial. Now, I need to go talk to Melinda, or our city is going to burn."

Brett puts a hand out. "She'll kill you. You'll die if you go in there."

"I have to try."

"Then, I'll go with you."

Paul shakes his head again. "No, I just need thirty minutes. After that, do what you came to do."

"You have fifteen minutes."

Paul nods, walks around the corner and into the garage. Behind him, Brett gives a hand signal, and a small team of agents makes themselves visible in the bushes and trees within view of the garage. He motions for all eyes to be on him. They'll be going in soon.

Melinda turns to Paul as he approaches. Her bodyguards already all have their weapons out and pointed at him. Paul holds his hands up as he approaches. Her eyes narrow at him.

"I know you," is all she says.

"I'm here to talk. I'm not armed." Paul says and does a slow turn for them to see.

Melinda nods to one of her team of guards, and they step forward to frisk Paul and make sure he's clean. When one of the guards give her a nod, she glares down at Paul.

"Speak." At her signal, the guards lower their weapons. "What do you want?"

"The drugs you are about to put on the streets are contaminated."

She raises a brow. "And how would you know that?"

"Check it."

Melinda hesitates for a breath, then signals for one of her cronies to come forward. He's obviously already strung out. She takes a packet from a stash on the table and slits the bag with a pocket knife, takes a bit from it, and holds it out for the strung out cronie to sniff desperately.

Then they all wait, and for a while, the cronie doesn't show any excessively abnormal behavior.

Melinda glares at Paul. "So, you risk your life coming here for noth—"

The cronie suddenly starts to strip, breaking out in heavy sweat. He gnaws on his skin as his clothes come off, his eyes bulging, starting to become bloodshot. Before anybody can do anything, he pulls his gun from his discarded clothes and starts to fire wildly, screaming as everybody takes cover.

A shot to the chest knocks the cronie to the ground, unconscious and twitching, bleeding from the wound. One bodyguard lowers the gun as a few others near the cronie.

Melinda's eyes narrow as she stares at the fallen cronie. It doesn't take long for her to regain her composure. "This changes nothing. To dispose of such a large shipment would be a loss to my company."

"Listen to yourself. You put this out on the streets, and this is what will happen to them. I know you at least care about the people."

"It's just business."

"Your business is this city. If it falls, your business falls. If you don't do the right thing, this city will burn."

"How would you know that?"

"I saw it."

Melinda stalks closer to Paul. "Let me tell you what I see. I see my drug sales going down because of you and your pastor friend who claims to heal the sick and raise the dead. I see you as a big problem. I see you being bad for business and a perfect opportunity has just fallen in my lap to erase an obvious problem. With all that you claim to do, I wonder if you can stop a bullet."

Paul stands his ground; the city is in danger, and she isn't seeing that. "This isn't you, Melinda. You're better than this."

Melinda scoffs at his face. "You know nothing about me, and you have sixty seconds to convince me not to kill you."

A bodyguard puts his finger to the trigger of his raised gun and clicks off the safety.

"I know you came here to be a light in the darkness, not to expand it. You have made some bad decisions, as I have, but it's not too late to change."

"Thirty seconds."

"What if you had the power to create the kind of world you want for your child? What would that look like?"

Melinda isn't even surprised that he knows, she just glares harder. "How do you know I have a child?"

"I can see her. I see her suffering as an adult because her mother didn't build a better world for her. If you had the power, what kind of world would you create on to her?"

Slowly, Melinda's hard exterior melts. "...not this..." she sighs.

"You can't change the future by making the same mistakes of the past, only by making different choices in the present."

Melinda toughens up again. "Ten seconds."

The bodyguard takes proper aim.

"Every human being born in this world will either add to the light or add to the darkness. My life is in your hands, the future we can create is in your hands, the fate of this city is in your hands."

Paul grabs Melinda's hand even as the bodyguard puts the gun to his head. The barrel is cold against his forehead, and he vaguely registers it as Melinda is propelled into the future.

*She stands on a mound, watching her city burn. There's chaos everywhere, people running amuck, killing each other, jumping from buildings, and horrors too much for her to look at.*

*In one hand, she's holding a torch, while her daughter grips the other hand tightly, the both of them watching what should have been the daughter's future burn to the ground.*

*Then, Melinda is sucked back through the matrix of time and into the realm outside of time, all the way back to her birth in the mind of God. Within the being of light, a small, lesser, light emerges and takes form. Soul Melinda stands before a light too potent for human eyes. From deep within this light, a voice emanates that seems to fill everything but is distinct enough to see a form standing within it.*

*The voice speaks to her. "Creation will emerge, but it will fall. Will you help to make it rise again?"*

*To this, she responds, "I will, Father."*

*To her right, she sees the lamb slain before the beginning of time by a priest. The blood flows down into the abyss of nothing and hits a formless globe, with no distinct form and covered in darkness.*

Melinda comes back to the present moment as a gunshot rings out. Paul grimaces but is unharmed. Melinda is holding the bodyguard's hand in the air as a trail of smoke emanates from his gun.

Paul releases Melinda's hand, and she crumbles to her knees. She struggles silently, calculating and recalculating in her head. Her cronies look confused and worried.

Just then, Brett and his men begin to file in, taking defensive positions with their guns drawn and pointed in the direction of Melinda and her men.

"Freeze! This is the police. Drop your weapons and put your hands on your head."

For a moment, everything seems to pause, but only for a moment. By the next moment, a shootout ensues, and Paul is dragged away by Melinda to where a vehicle is parked behind and away from all the gunfire.

"Surrender, Melinda. There is no way out."

"Not yet," she replies, flicking her thumb in thought. "There is something I think I should do first."

"We're in the middle of a gunfight."

"Follow me."

Melinda leads Paul through a maze of containers and to a hidden door.

Paul and Melinda make it out of the industrial park while the gunfire continues to ring out, and Paul points to John's car, and they make for it instead.

"What's going on—" John starts to ask.

"Go, John. Just go!"

Hurriedly, John drives off, not very sure what's happening or where he's going.

In the industrial park, the gunfire ceases, and all of Melinda's men are down, some of them lay haphazardly, moaning in pain and nursing gunshot wounds. Some of them are completely unconscious. The officers start to go round, handcuffing them and helping the emergency services carry the wounded to the ambulances.

Brett walks around, searching for Melinda. An officer emerges from the back. "We've searched the entire premises. They're not here."

Frustrated, Brett kicks over a table of drugs.

"Burn it all!"

# SEVENTEEN

At the pool house, Melinda is in the pool with John. It's the same one Paul had been baptized in. Paul is on his phone. When he's done, he hangs up.

"I've been having dreams," Melinda says, "hearing voices, but I was too deep into what I was doing, I couldn't see a way that didn't involve death or going to jail…but then, you showed up." The last bit is said to Paul.

"We don't have much time," he says instead.

John clears his throat. The excitement and shock of this moment makes his voice shake when he speaks. "Melinda, will you renounce the world to follow Jesus?"

Paul folds his arms and watches.

"I do."

John pulls her down into the pool, and time again slows as a being of light hits Melinda's body, igniting blue flames as she emerges from the pool.

"…come Holy Spirit…"

A dove-like being appears above Melinda and is absorbed by the blue flames, becoming one with her body as John leads her out of the pool.

Paul's eyes narrow as he sees Melinda seemingly begin to duplicate. Light bodies emerge from her physical body, forming almost a ladder going up, multiplying in the heavens, all the way through the matrix and into the realm of light.

He'd known what was going to happen the moment John had asked her if she was going to accept Jesus, but this...he hadn't expected something like this. "That's new!" he exclaims.

*In the realm of light, Melinda is standing before a row of thrones that extend beyond sight in all directions. There is a seat with her name etched on it. Others are being shown to their seat, but Melinda hesitates before taking her place on her throne.*

At the pool house, Melinda dries her hair with a towel, and Paul's watches as her light duplicates all around him and fades into an unknown reality.

"I still feel the same," Melinda exclaims.

Paul shakes his head, the vision still reverberating inside him. "Oh, far from it."

In the distance, sirens become audible, and they grow louder every moment.

John smiles at Melinda brightly. "A new chapter in your life begins now, Melinda."

Melinda scoffs at him good-naturedly. "I never thought that was possible. I guess now when I die, I'll be going to heaven."

"Actually, you're already there."

Moments later, the sirens finally catch up. John and Paul watch as Melinda is handcuffed and put into the back of a patrol car. She looks back at them when the car begins to drive off; she looks until the car disappears into the distance.

They are still watching the street the car disappeared into when Brett comes over. "You two could be in a hell of a lot of trouble for aiding and abetting a known fugitive," he starts, "but, I'll let it slide, just this once. Consider us even." He flexes his new hand and walks away.

"Not by a long shot," Paul says under his breath.

Brett's head whips back, he frowns at them. "I heard that. Stay out of trouble you two."

# EIGHTEEN

"*There is a world that we can see and touch, but it's a mistake to think of that as our only reality...*"

At the Tselem Fellowship, a sign is being hoisted up above the entrance of the sleeping area. The sign reads *Grace Williams Institute*.

John helps a woman, who has been badly beaten, to a bed. When Paul touches her, her wounds begin to heal instantly.

"*...this physical world is only a small fraction, a very small fraction, of the worlds of which we are a part. We are perpetually in the company of the seen and unseen...*"

One of the hands that Paul uses to heal people now has a thick, gold wedding band on it; it's his left hand.

"*...angels and men in white phase in and out of physical reality, ever-present...*"

The woman that was injured before, now looking a lot better, sits up.

"*...the Father created a world for all. A world as vast and immeasurable as eternity itself. We can choose to settle* *and build our own little world on a small planet called earth, but we were created for much more. So much more..."*

Into the institute, Cher pushes a baby stroller. On one of her hands too is another golden wedding band.

John coos at the child in the stroller. "There's my godson." Cher gives him the stroller and goes to wrap her arms around Paul, kissing him.

Lily comes carrying a box of donuts and a gallon carton of coffee. She's pregnant. John kisses her and gets on his knees to check on the bun in the oven.

In a prison cell, Melinda sits on her bed with her back against the wall, reading a Bible.

*"...In the beginning, the world was covered in darkness. When the Father spoke, He said, "Let there be light." We are the light of the world. You, me, all of us..."*

In the prison chapel, Melinda stands on the stage to preach, speaking passionately to the inmates, baptizing some of them in the bathroom. She's smiling as she spreads the word and even glowing a perfect spiritual light that starts to steadily infect those she preaches to.

In the pool in town, John also baptizes more members of the community. By the pool side, volunteers stand with towels to hand out. There are long lines of people waiting to be baptized.

*"...while we are here on earth, we must know that our light extends from here, all the way back to eternity, and to the very Being from which we were birthed..."*

Through galaxies, through the universe, through the realm of nothing, through the matrix of time and eternity, into the realm of light where angels, spirits, and souls gather looking down on the earth and into all the created realms.

The earth, they all see, is covered in a dark shroud, but small specks of light are breaking forth and beginning to expand, replacing the darkness with orbs and circles of light. Cheviel is among the angels looking down. She smiles and flies off.

*"...God didn't just want human beings to be real in His mind, He wanted you to be real in creation. Without being born into creation, you do not influence it, and if there is no one in the image and likeness of God in creation, then creation will cease to exist. The Father built this world for all. The creation of the heavens and earth is God's gift to humanity, His son..."*

Greyson, Paul's son, is five years old now. Paul kisses his forehead and smiles down at his angelic face.

"...so, one day, you will rule nations, my son, because you were created to be great. We all were."

In John's house, they're all gathered and sitting around the dinner table. Delicious-looking food and non-alcoholic drinks are laid out, Paul bows his head and closes his eyes, and leads everybody in prayer.

As his hands connect with John's and Lily's, Paul is sucked into a vision.

*Paul is pulled out of his body, pulled through the roof of the house above the neighborhood, above the earth, above the galaxies, all the way out in uncreated light that appears like deep galaxies.*

*He sees the created world, the discovered galaxies, like an eye, but he goes further away, all the created world coming into view, undecipherable. As it comes into view, it begins to move, and expand and twist, taking shape like a large cloud unfolding on itself. It begins to take shape, its interior swirling with varying colors and hues, creating a breath-taking view. Paul's eyes widen as the huge vortex and void take the form of a man...*

*The created world, known and unknown, shaped like a...human being...*

*The feature of his face is unrecognizable at first, but its details take form and the human being's identity comes into view. A universe, alive, moving, shifting, growing, now with a face...Paul's own face... it takes a deep breath. Its eyes snap open, life vibrating through its interior, absorbing life from an unknown, unseen source much bigger than itself.*

Paul's eyes snap open. He's back in the dining room with John and the rest. He's sitting next to John and Lily, connecting both. His eyes remain wide, his expression confused, as the vision fades. His grip on them loosens, but he stays connected.

Paul watches as his hand starts to glow with a blue flame, which is passed on to the others who also begin to glow. The flame moves up their hands and engulfs their entire bodies, turning each of them into a divine flame as their entire bodies are bathed with fire.

The flames fade away as they open their eyes and begin to eat. John notices Paul's pale and awed expression.

"What? Did you see something?"

Paul can't say what he's seen. For years to come, he will not be able to articulate what he has seen.

*It is not yet revealed to us what we will be. We know that, however, when it is revealed, we will be just like Him, for we will see Him just as He is. We will only because, beloved, we are children of God.*

Printed in Great Britain
by Amazon